THERE WAS NO MISTAKING . . .

Somebody *was* inside that ship. Omigosh! We had to get him out fast! I reached for a rag to protect my hands from the hot bottle, but before my fingers had even wrapped around it there was a gigantic *pop!*, and the cork burst from the bottle and flew across the room. Following right behind it, a tiny man, no taller than about half my thumb, jumped down from the bottle onto my laboratory table. And boy, was he *furious!*

Miss Switch
To The Rescue

Barbara Brooks Wallace

ILLUSTRATED BY
KATHLEEN GARRY McCORD

AN ARCHWAY PAPERBACK
Published by POCKET BOOKS • NEW YORK

Front cover photograph copyright © 1981 American Broadcasting Companies, Inc., from ABC's Weekend Special "Miss Switch to the Rescue."

An Archway Paperback published by
POCKET BOOKS, a Simon & Schuster Division of
GULF & WESTERN CORPORATION
1230 Avenue of the Americas, New York, N.Y. 10020

Copyright © 1981 by Abingdon

Published by arrangement with Abingdon
Library of Congress Catalog Card Number: 81-10916

ISBN: 0-671-43848-4

First Archway Paperback printing April, 1982

10 9 8 7 6 5 4 3 2

AN ARCHWAY PAPERBACK and colophon are
trademarks of Simon & Schuster.

Printed in the U.S.A.

IL 3+

For my cousins
Johnny, Jenny, and Mary Jackson
This book, with love

CONTENTS

Miss Switch
To The Rescue

1

Two Last Roses of Summer

"Boring!" my friend Amelia Daley said.

"It sure is!" I replied.

I was sitting on the floor, propped up against my bed, watching the leafless branches of our oak tree sway mournfully in the fierce February storm. There was just enough light from my room to give them a spooky glow. Swish! Swish! Swish! A branch scraped across the window like the fingers of an old skeleton.

"Boring!" repeated Amelia. She was sitting at my desk, staring gloomily at the stump of one of my favorite chewed-up pencils.

"Boring, *boring!*" I replied with a deep sigh.

We had been pursuing a conversation along these lines for some time, and who knows how much longer it would have continued if my mother hadn't appeared in my room just then.

My room, for those of you who may not have read an earlier account of myself (written by me), is actually a very interesting place to be. This is because I've become a great scientist recently, and even though I don't have exactly what you'd call an honest-to-goodness laboratory, I do have a lot of neat scientific stuff in my room.

There's my microscope, of course, but I also have a bunch of things I made myself, like containers made from used light bulbs, a graduated cylinder from an olive bottle, and small pans from lids of preserving jars. I even have an alcohol lamp I made from a mustard jar, and a tripod that used to be a tomato can. That's to put over the alcohol lamp.

Amelia, who has recently become a great scientist herself, thinks all this stuff is pretty nifty, too. So you can probably understand that when we were talking about something being boring, it was not my room we were talking about.

"What's wrong with you children?" my mother asked cheerfully. "You look like the two last roses of summer."

I gave my mother a look of disgust. Two last roses of summer! The only correct thing about that statement was the "two." Summer ended six months ago, and I've never heard of any roses lasting until the middle of February. How unscientific can you get!

"We're just thinking about how boring school is now, Mrs. Brown," said Amelia.

2

My mother looked surprised. "Why, how could school be boring when you have as fine a teacher as Mrs. Fitzgerald? I thought you liked her, Rupert."

"Oh, I like her all right. And I guess she's a pretty good teacher, but—but—"

"But she's not Miss Switch!" Amelia finished for me.

"Miss Switch?" said my mother dimly. "You mean the Miss Switch who was your teacher for a short time when you started fifth grade last fall?"

"That's the one!" I said.

My mother was puzzled. "Well, I know you liked her a great deal, but my goodness, I'm sure she didn't make school any more interesting than Mrs. Fitzgerald."

Oh? Amelia and I exchanged raised-eyebrow glances. The truth was that no ordinary teacher, no matter how nice she was or how hard she tried, could make school as interesting as Miss Switch.

What teacher, for instance, could make a spitball fly back without any visible means of projection, and hit the person who sent it? How could an ordinary teacher cause a quarterback and a football to disappear in a football game, making for the most unusual game in history? And most of all, how could any ordinary teacher take you on a broomstick ride (no engine, no batteries, no fooling!) to meet with a

3

crazy (but scientifically mind-boggling) contraption called a Comput-o-witch?

You can take it from me, Rupert P. (for Peevely, though that's not something I care to have generally breezed around) Brown III, scientist devoted to truth and accuracy, that that's what happened with Miss Switch. Because the fact is that only one side of Miss Switch's nature was that of a teacher. The other side, known only to Amelia and me, was that of a witch. *A real one!* And naturally, a person who combines all the best qualities of a terrific teacher and a good witch would be pretty impossible to beat.

I think you can understand, however, why I could not reveal all this to my mother or my father. My father thinks he is a very humorous person and probably would have come up with a bunch of jokes about the subject, not believing any of it for a moment. My mother would have rushed me off to our doctor for a physical, or loaded me down with vitamin C. My mother has simple remedies for everything. Some of them actually work. But I just don't believe vitamin C is the answer to witchcraft.

So Amelia and I said no more as my mother went to the window and peered out. "Brrr! It's a nasty night. That must be why you two are feeling so glum. See here, have you finished your homework for tomorrow?"

Amelia and I looked at one another again and

4

shrugged. We didn't know what this was leading up to. Then we both nodded. We had finished our homework ages ago.

"Good!" my mother said. "We don't want Amelia getting behind on her work so her parents won't ever let her stay with us again, do we?"

Amelia and I shook our heads dutifully. No, we certainly didn't want that. I should explain here that Amelia was spending a few days with us because her mother and father had to make an emergency trip out of town. She slept in the small room down the hall that is our guest room when we have guests, and my mother's sewing room when we don't.

"Then why don't you take this hour before bedtime and start on one of your experiments, Rupert? That should cheer you both up."

My mother was really feeling sorry for us. Neither of my parents ever actually suggests that I do an experiment. This is because a lot of them end up looking diseased and disgusting (like my moldy-orange experiment), or smelling terrible (like my maggot-growing-on-porkchop experiment, which looks diseased and disgusting besides). Some of them, especially ones involving my mustard-jar alcohol burner, my parents seem to think are downright dangerous, as well as smelling terrible. My father says if the smells haven't already driven us out of the house, we will probably all be blown out some day. He really does think he is funny. At any rate, you can understand my surprise at hearing this suggestion from my mother.

"We'll think about it," I replied, and tried to look pleased and grateful.

My mother then left with a cheerful, encouraging, sympathetic, hopeful smile. But as soon as she had disappeared, Amelia and I fell into another gloomy silence.

"I just don't feel like doing an experiment," I said.

"I don't either," said Amelia.

"I wonder why we don't?"

"Maybe it's because we've suddenly started thinking so hard about Miss Switch."

"Maybe you're right."

We fell silent again. "Do you suppose it's because she's getting ready to come back?" Amelia asked suddenly.

I shook my head. "She said she was never going to, and I believe her."

"Well, maybe somebody repaired that dumb old Comput-o-witch, and it's sending Miss Switch back here to prove herself as a witch all over again. Did you ever think of that, Rupert P. Brown?" Amelia's brown curls bounced defiantly on her forehead. She was getting mad at me, as if it was all my fault.

"Of course I've thought of that!" I got angry too. "But when I say that the Comput-o-witch was wrecked, I mean it was r-u-i-n-e-d, *wrecked*,

6

Amelia M. Daley! And anyway, the only witch who would have wanted to repair it was Saturna, whose idea it was in the first place. Which, in case you've forgotten, is why she was banished from Witch's Mountain. The rest of the witches hated it.''

"Well then—well then—" Amelia was not going to give up. "Don't you remember that Miss Switch said that sometimes when the moon is full and the night is clear, we might see a single cloud pass overhead, and that cloud could be *her?*"

"What do you mean, don't I remember that? Gee, Amelia, how many times have we stood gazing up at the moon this winter hoping to see Miss Switch? Once I almost got pneumonia!"

"That was just a stiff neck, Rupert."

"Well, it *felt* like pneumonia." I wasn't being very scientific, but sometimes when you get pushed too far, you forget yourself. "Anyway, what's that got to do with anything?"

"What it has to do with, Rupert, is maybe Miss Switch is going to fly over tonight and wants us to be sure and see her."

"That would be a very good possibility except for two things, Amelia. One, it isn't a clear night. Two, there's no moon."

"I don't care. I'm going to look anyway!" Amelia flung herself out of the desk chair and ran to the window.

What could I do but follow? I mean, what if

7

she was right? We pressed our noses against the cold window pane, staring upward through the weaving oak tree branches into the sky. But it was soon clear that we weren't going to see anything outside my window except bare tree branches dancing spookily in the howling wind, and an inky-black sky. The closest thing we saw to a moon was the lonely, eerie-looking street lamp at the foot of our driveway.

"There, you see, I told you there'd be nothing." I said it angrily to hide my disappointment. I really had wanted Amelia to be right.

"Well—well—" Amelia was close to tears.

"Look," I said quickly, "this wasn't such a bad idea. We both know that with witchcraft, lots of weird things are possible. The storm *could* have suddenly ended and the moon *could* have come out. That just didn't happen this time. But we'll see Miss Switch again one day. I know we will!"

Amelia gave me a watery smile.

"Anyway," I said, "why don't we do what Mom suggested? I have this neat experiment I've been wanting to try. Come on!"

But Amelia didn't answer. She had her nose pressed up tightly against the windowpane again, and beckoned to me excitedly.

"What is it?"

"Look, Rupert, over there by the juniper bushes beside your driveway. There's a strange shadow, and it just moved!"

8

"It's probably just the bushes blowing around in the wind," I said, but I peered out the window anyway. And what I saw instead of the normal two bushes was *three* bushes. Or was it a bush?

Amelia and I turned to one another and breathed the words together, *"Miss Switch!"*

"But if it is Miss Switch, what would she be doing skulking around our house?" I said. "I would think she'd just show up in our classroom the way she did before."

Amelia shrugged. "She might be in trouble again and need to see us in a hurry."

"Maybe. But what if it isn't Miss Switch? What if it's a—a burglar looking for a way in?"

Amelia gasped, and I quickly switched off the lamp so we could see out but not be seen at the window. We didn't wait long before the third shadow, the one that was *not* the juniper bush, separated itself from the other two and slithered across the driveway toward our house. This seemed downright slinky and sinister. What should we do? Run down and warn my family? My mind was spinning. And then the doorbell rang.

Now, a burglar does not ordinarily ring the doorbell to announce that he is about to rob your house. On the other hand, the shadow did not seem to be your normal, everyday kind of visitor. Which could only mean one thing.

"It *is* Miss Switch!" cried Amelia.

9

"It's got to be!" I said.

We tore from the room and thumped down the stairs. Racing past the living room door, I noted that my parents were deep in a game of Scrabble, with the stereo turned up full force playing one of my father's favorite operas. The soprano hollering at the top of her lungs had drowned out the sound of the bell so they hadn't even heard it, nor seen us race by the door. So it was just Amelia and I who threw the door open to greet Miss Switch.

Except that it wasn't Miss Switch! Not by a long, long, *long* shot. My stomach still shrivels up into a cold knot, and my skin prickles with goose bumps even now when I think of the person who *was* there, standing right outside our doorway!

2

A Strange Delivery

The person in our doorway was a woman, although it was difficult to tell this at first glance. Her face was hidden deep inside a musty, ancient black cloak, which covered her like a shroud and gave off a curious smell of soot. The light from our doorway, however, was just enough to pick up a huge nose the color of moldy green cheese, covered wall-to-wall with the nastiest-looking hairy warts I had ever seen in my life. My most disgusting experiments could not have held a candle to that nose. The light also picked up two evil pinpricks of eyes that glittered inside dark, deep sockets, and a mouth spread open (I think this was supposed to represent a friendly smile) to reveal five grim-looking yellow teeth, three above, two below.

Altogether, this was not my idea of the kind of person you would want arriving on your doorstep on a dark, moonless night. Or a sunny day, either. I grabbed Amelia by the hand. "W-w-wait a minute. I'll go tell my mother and father you're here. Th-th-they'll be glad to see you!"

Before I'd even finished the sentence, a bony hand flicked out from the cloak and snapped around my arm. "Sssssstay!" Her voice sounded hot and gravelly, as if it had been filtered through burning charcoal.

She removed her hand from around my arm, but v-e-e-ery slowly to let me know she could get it back there again in a hurry. Then she flashed another yellow smile at Amelia and me. "I didn't come to see your parents, Rupert. I came to see you and your little friend, Amelia, here." She put her face up close enough to mine that I could feel her hot breath. "I wouldn't run and tell them anything, deary. Better for you if you don't, eh?"

I couldn't agree with her more. I could still feel the effect of that bony hand around my arm, and there was nothing to say I wouldn't feel it around my neck. I confess that I considered hollering, but I wasn't certain I could out-holler the soprano doing her best in our living room. So, being a reasonable fellow, I simply nodded.

"Good! I thought you'd see it my way. Anyway, what would be the point of telling your parents anything? I've only come to give you a little present. All children like presents.

You'd like a little present, wouldn't you, deary?'' This question was addressed to Amelia, accompanied by another nasty, yellow-toothed leer.

Amelia turned to me with eyes the size of large bottle caps. I gave her a quick nod, letting her know that "yes" was a safer answer than "no." After all, we didn't want to make anyone angry.

"Y-y-yes." Amelia's voice was quavering as much as mine.

"Sssplendid!" hissed the witch.

Yes, I said "witch." I had suspected this from the first, but a scientist does not jump to instant conclusions. I had to feel pretty well convinced before I was ready to reveal this information.

She dived inside her cloak and rummaged around for something. Then her bony hand darted out and thrust a tattered package, about the size of a shoe box, tied with string, into my hand. I just stood and stared at it, wondering what we were expected to do next. After all, this was not your normal, everyday, United Parcel delivery. "Sh-sh-should we open it now?" I asked.

"Oh no! You take it up to your room, dearies. You can open it there. I *expect* you to open it there. But I have to warn you about something." The witch's voice became low and menacing. "Don't show this package or its contents

13

to anyone. Do you hear me? *Anyone!* It could be very—unhealthy for you. I hesitate to tell you *how* unhealthy. Do I make myself clear?''

Boy, did she make herself clear! "Y-y-yes," I stammered.

She rubbed her bony hands together. "Very good! I can see that you are smart children, and that I can trust you not to do anything—foolish. Now, run along and enjoy yourselves. And mind what I've said, dearies. Eh?" With a wild cackle, she whirled around, her black cloak billowing out like the smoke from a witch's cauldron. A moment later, she had melted into the darkness.

I took a deep swallow to get rid of the scared, dry lump in my throat. "Come on!" I croaked. "Let's get back upstairs, Amelia."

We crept past the living room, where my mother and father were still peacefully playing their game of Scrabble, with nothing worse on their minds than maybe what to do with two T's, an N, an X, and no vowels. How could they have missed all that had happened at the front door, even with the soprano making all that racket? It had to be witchcraft, I told myself. After all, I knew quite a bit about the subject already. I shivered as we tiptoed swiftly and silently up the stairs. Witchcraft!

Safely in my room, we quietly locked the door. This is not normally allowed by my parents, I presume because it would keep them

14

from getting in quickly if I should ever blow myself to bits with one of my experiments. But in light of the witch's instructions, we had no choice. We had to open the package in secrecy.

I set it down carefully on my bed. Then Amelia and I sat down equally carefully on either side of it. Our eyes were riveted to that tattered package tied in a bedraggled piece of string. It looked spooky, but maybe it contained nothing worse than some dried bats' wings or toadstools, or maybe a jar of homemade pickled eye of newt. Maybe the witch was really a nice person who just wanted to give us a present. Or so I tried to tell myself. I really wasn't fooling myself for a moment. Right then I would have traded every piece of my valuable scientific equipment for just five seconds of X-ray vision.

Amelia drew her arms around herself, and shuddered. "We—we're going to have to open it, Rupert." Her voice was trembling.

"I—I know." My voice wasn't exactly steady either.

I hesitated. Then, with my heart jumping around somewhere in the region of my throat, I reached out gingerly and tugged a loose end of the knot that held the string. To my surprise, the knot pulled apart easily. Slowly and carefully, I peeled away the ragged, brown paper to reveal a plain, ordinary, cardboard box. It was stained and darkened with age, but there

15

were no markings on it to give away what might be hidden inside. Then, slowly and carefully, I lifted the lid. And gasped!

Inside the box, lying on a bed of crumpled rags, was a glass bottle with a wide mouth capped by a blackened cork stopper. And inside the bottle, floating on a tiny sea of water, was a little ship. It was modeled after the old-fashioned wood sailing ships that used to cross the seas long before anyone even *heard* of a steam engine. I took off my glasses and wiped them on my bedspread before replacing them on my nose, so I could get a clearer look at the neat little wooden hull, the tiny, polished poop-deck, and the trim sails not much bigger than large postage stamps. There was even a terrific miniature figurehead on the prow of the ship.

"Oh, Rupert!" Amelia breathed. "She *was* a good witch, after all."

"Heart like a marshmallow," I said, attempting a little humor.

"Why do you suppose she gave it to us?" Amelia asked.

"Beats me," I replied.

"Rupert, do you suppose it would be all right to take the ship out of the bottle so we could look at it more closely?" Amelia's eyes were sparkling.

"Hmmm!" I hummed, rubbing my chin and studying the contents of the box. "Hmmm!"

There was some very interesting-looking

stuff sitting around on the quarterdeck, like a compass and a navigator's chart, and I was itching to study some of it under a microscope. And maybe we might even find some miniature gold doubloons hidden away in the hold! But, marshmallow heart aside, what if the bottle was booby-trapped? "Hmmm!" I repeated.

"Oh, Rupert!" Without waiting for my thoughtful opinion, Amelia lifted the bottle from the box. And nothing more happened than that the little ship bobbed gently in its small sea.

At this point, my scientific care and caution flew out the window. I grabbed the bottle from Amelia and, without even thinking about the possible danger of removing the cork from the bottle, began to twist and tug at it. But the cork didn't budge. Then Amelia took a turn at twisting and tugging. The little ship pitched and rocked, but the cork remained as tightly stuck as if someone had glued it in. We set the bottle back in the box and glumly watched the bobbing ship come quietly to rest in the small body of water.

Water? What was there about water? I thought. Then I slapped my forehead and practically slid right off the bed. How could I, Rupert P. Brown III, great scientist, have overlooked a solution to opening the bottle that was sitting there and staring me right in the face?

But before I could get a word out, Amelia

turned to me, her forehead creased by a deep frown. "Rupert, I just this minute thought of a principle of science we could use to get the cork out. If we could heat the water in the bottle enough to make it steam, the steam would expand and pop the cork out. Do you think that would work?"

Boy, talk about your great scientific minds running in the same great scientific circles! Or—or was it—witchcraft? Well, who cared? "Wow, Amelia! I was thinking the same thing you were, and I sure do think it would work."

"But how are we going to heat the water, Rupert? I don't think we ought to do it on the stove. What if your mother or father came into the kitchen?"

"Don't worry. Leave everything to me!" I pointed to my mustard-jar alcohol lamp and to-mato-can tripod. "Abracadabra!"

It took us only a few moments to light the lamp and lay the bottle over it on the tomato-can tripod. With chins on our hands, and elbows resting on my lab table (which happens to be an old card table where I keep my laboratory stuff), we watched the flame dance under the bottle. Soon, small bubbles began to form and rise up through the water. The bottle began to fill with clouds of steam, and, within a few seconds, the glass was so fogged up we could hardly see the little ship inside it.

"You don't think the hot water will hurt the ship, do you, Rupert?" Amelia asked me anxiously.

"It might if it were going to be in there a long time. But it will be only a couple of minutes, and it looks like a pretty sturdy little ship. Anyway, it's not as if there were somebody inside the ship getting cooked."

"Ugh!" said Amelia.

The water inside the bottle bubbled like a steaming teakettle. The fog grew thicker and thicker. The ship disappeared from view entirely. Then all at once, mixed with the bubbling sounds of the water inside the bottle, came sounds that curiously resembled human coughing, wheezing, and sputtering. Startled, Amelia and I looked at each other, and then put our ears closer to the bottle.

Cough! Wheeze! Sputter! "What in thunderation is going on in here! Help! I'm going to be cooked to death! Help!"

We couldn't see a thing inside that bottle, but there was no mistaking the fact now that somebody *was* inside that ship, and *going* to be cooked. Omigosh! We had to get him out fast! I reached for a rag to protect my hands from the hot bottle, but before my fingers had even wrapped around it, there was a gigantic *pop!*

19

and the cork burst from the bottle and flew across the room. Following right behind it, a tiny man, no taller than about half my thumb, jumped down from the bottle onto my laboratory table. And boy, was he *furious!*

3

Mordo

I didn't blame the little man. I had to admit I'd be pretty mad, too, if someone put my place of residence on the stove and tried to cook me out of it. "W-w-we're sorry," I stammered.

"W-w-we really are!" echoed Amelia.

But the small man acted as if he hadn't heard us. He went right on stomping angrily around the table, drops of water flying off from his tall, black boots. Thump! Thump! Bang! "Ruined my best boots! Thunderation! Murderation! Blast!" he roared. Bang! Bang! Thump!

While he was storming around the table, my brain did some quick calculating. From my readings about what usually came locked up in bottles, I concluded that this was probably a genie. Oh, I knew that genies ordinarily came floating out dressed in robes and turbans like some kind of far-Eastern potentate. But who was to say that a genie could not be an inch-

tall, old sea captain, with grizzled hair and apple-red cheeks, who stomped instead of floated out of a bottle?

And if he was a genie, which I strongly believed, there was one thing Amelia and I could probably count on. That was to have three wishes granted. The dream of my life (and I guess everyone else's in the world)—*THREE WISHES!* My warm feelings toward the witch who had given us the bottle grew even warmer. What a present—wow!

The genie didn't look, however, as if he were ever going to quit ranting and raving and carrying on all over my lab table. I was getting impatient to move on with what looked like a pretty exciting evening. Stomp! Stomp! Thump! Bang! I was getting tired of it.

"Look," I said finally in a firm voice, "we *said* we were sorry."

"Both of us," said Amelia, just as firmly.

"Sorry won't fix these boots if they're ruined," retorted the sea captain/genie. "Besides, you two almost fried me alive in that bottle!"

"Boiled," I corrected him (to keep the record scientifically straight).

"Fried! Boiled! What's the difference? The point is you almost cooked my goose, the goose of Captain Mordecai!" He shook his fist at us. This captain, though twinkly-eyed, was a pretty crusty character.

23

"We didn't know you were on the ship," Amelia said.

"You should have guessed!" bellowed the captain. "Who do you think kept her shining and shipshape all these centuries?"

Amelia and I just shrugged. We hadn't thought about that.

"Hmmmph!" the captain snorted.

But I, at least, had noticed the word "centuries," which further strengthened my belief that Captain Mordecai was a genie. Who else could survive for centuries inside a bottle except a genie? And I had noticed something else. Whereas the captain had been no more than one inch tall when he jumped out of the bottle, he was now three inches tall. I blinked, and he seemed to have grown to five inches. Didn't genies expand like balloons once they had escaped from captivity? Wasn't this another proof? Or—or was I just *imagining* it?

"Excuse me, please, Captain Mordecai." I was very polite, because I certainly didn't want to make him any madder than he already was. "Are you, by any chance, growing?"

"By any chance I am certainly *not* growing!" he snapped.

"You are too!" Amelia snapped right back. "You're a lot bigger than when you came out of the bottle."

"Nonsense!" roared the captain.

But it was not nonsense, since Amelia and

I were seeing the same thing. It was proof positive that I was not losing (a) my eyesight, or (b) my wits. A few blinks later, and the captain was over two feet tall. He jumped onto the floor. Ker-thunk! Then, almost as if a bolt of lightning had shot right through him from head to toe, he suddenly grew to at least six-foot-six!

"Aaahhh!" He lifted his arms to stretch and practically filled my whole room.

Now, the captain had lied to us, and I didn't like it very much. I wanted to tell him what I thought of this, but I have to be honest. Lecturing someone six-feet-six-inches tall is a little different from lecturing someone one inch tall. At any rate, as I remembered it, some genies could be pretty sensitive, and this one seemed to be more so than most. I didn't want to make him so angry he wouldn't do what he was supposed to do; grant us those three wishes. If he wanted us to think he was still an inch tall, that was all right with me. I raised an eyebrow at Amelia to let her know we had better not argue with him.

"Captain Mordecai, sir," I said, craning my neck back so far I almost fell over, "we apologize. We were wrong. You haven't grown any. But I have to tell you that I know you're a genie. Also, my mother or father might be in here at any minute to tell us it's time for bed, and if they find you here, I don't know what will happen. So if you're going to grant us our three wishes, Captain Mordecai, genie, sir, I would like to suggest respectfully that you get on with it.''

"Three wishes, is it? *THREE WISHES!* Ho! Ho! Ho! Ha! Ha! Ha! Hee! Hee! Hee!'' Captain Mordecai's laughter rolled around my room like thunder. If it didn't reach my parents in the living room, it must have been because the soprano was hollering again.

"Genie, is it?'' he roared. "I'll genie the *two* of *you!*''

Then right before Amelia's and my very eyes, Captain Mordecai began to change from a crusty, though twinkly-eyed, old sea captain, into something far, far different.

His eyes turned suddenly from a bright sea-blue to a deadly coal-black, with sparks actually shooting right out of them. His grizzled hair grew dark and long, and his apple-red cheeks faded into a gruesome grey-green. His captain's uniform seemed to melt away into a grim, long black gown and cloak.

"Wh-wh-where is Captain Mordecai?'' I stammered, my tongue practically glued to the roof of my mouth with fright.

"And wh-wh-who are you?'' quavered Amelia.

"I *am* Captain Mordecai, alias Mordo the warlock, out of that blasted bottle at last, and free as a bat, thanks to your clever little minds! But lest you think yourselves too clever,'' he

26

narrowed his eyes at us threateningly, "let me tell you something. I knew all along I was growing bigger, and bigger, and *BIGGER*. You thought I was a little silly in the head, eh? Well, for your information, as long as I was smaller than you were, you could have wished me back in that bottle at any time. What do you think of that, eh?" he repeated, snarling at us.

What I thought was that I was beginning not to like the looks of this. After all, a six-foot-six evil warlock is a lot different kind of present from a nifty little one-inch sea captain, even if he is crusty and has a bad temper. I have to admit, my warm feelings for the witch who brought us the present were rapidly cooling.

"Well," Mordo snorted, "at least you did what you were supposed to do. *She* said your little scientific brains would figure a way, and we could kill two birds with one pop of a cork!"

"Wh-wh-who is *she?*" asked Amelia, which happened to be my question exactly. "Is—is *she* the witch who brought you?"

"That's none of your business!" snapped Mordo.

I didn't quite agree with him, but I didn't think it would do much good to say so. I decided to proceed to another subject.

"Wh-wh-what do you mean about killing two birds with one pop of a cork? W-w-will you tell us that?"

"Glad to oblige," sneered Mordo, with a

sweeping bow. "The first bird was getting me out of that bottle, which is something *you* did for *me*. The second bird is something *I'm* going to do for *you!*"

Something told me that what he was going to do for us was not nearly so nice as what we had done for him. "Wh-wh-what?" I asked. I could feel my tonsils quivering.

"Ah yes, 'what' indeed! Well, it happens that what I'm going to do for the two of you is turn you into—*toads!*" Mordo threw back his head and rocked with horrible laughter.

"T-T-TOADS!" Amelia and I cried.

"B-b-but why?" Amelia asked.

"Oh, it's just something I promised *her* I'd do if you got me out of the bottle. Turning people into toads used to be my specialty, you know," Mordo added conversationally, as if we were sitting around talking about a change in the weather.

"W-w-we didn't know that," I said, which was certainly the truth. Then I took a deep swallow. "Wh-wh-when are you planning to do this?"

"Now, of course! You'll have to give me a few moments to think this over, however." Mordo rubbed his sharp, ugly chin with his sharp, ugly hand. "It's been a long time since I've done one of these toad changes."

"T-t-take your time!" I said.

Amelia and I looked at each other helplessly.

What could we do, make a dash for it? We'd never get halfway across the room to the door we had carefully locked. I began to see the point of my mother and father's rule about locked doors.

I looked accusingly at my lab table. Where was science now when I needed it? As far back as I could dig in my mind, I couldn't find one single fact that would help keep Amelia and me from turning into toads. *Toads!* I thought with a shudder. I could almost feel my skin turning green and lumpy, my mouth growing wider and wider, and my whole body shrinking. Oh, help! Our only hope was that Mordo had forgotten his old specialty. But that hope was soon smashed.

"Aha!" he snarled at us. "It's come back to me now." He started to mutter a bunch of weird incantations and swoop around the room, his black gown swirling around his ankles and his cloak flying out and knocking everything over on my lab table. Soon there would be nothing left in one piece for my parents to remember me by.

"W-w-watch out!" I hollered. "You're going to wreck all my scientific stuff!"

"A pox on your scientific stuff!" shrieked Mordo. "The way you're going to end up, you won't need it!" He never missed a beat, but went right on swooping and swooshing around my room.

Amelia and I, however, didn't so much as develop a wart. We stayed the same size and, what is more important, the same shape.

"Blast!" exploded Mordo angrily. "It's just been too long, and I must have lost my touch. But don't you two start celebrating. I'm simply going to have to take you back to my century, and *there* we'll see what we shall see!"

"Oh, no!" I announced. "Y-y-you're not taking us anywhere!"

Mordo bared his teeth at us. "And what's to stop me?"

Looking around my room desperately, I spotted something I'd forgotten all about. "This!" I shouted, and snatched up my saxophone.

"Wh-what's that?" stammered Mordo, cringing.

"It's a—a *Saxophonius gruesomus*," I replied, boldly waving the saxophone under his nose. "It has some terrible powers. And if you don't believe me, just ask the Head Witch at Witch's Mountain about it!"

"The Head Witch at Witch's Mountain?" Mordo was clearly impressed with this piece of information.

"That's right!" Amelia chimed in. *"She'll* tell you!"

To be sure Mordo got the point, I waved the saxophone under his nose again, and then blew a couple of my usual weird, out-of-tune, sour notes right into his ear.

30

"Aaaargh!" he snarled, clapping his hands over his ears. Then he dropped his eyelids until his eyes were no more than evil slits. "I guess I'll just have to try a different tack then, won't I? I'll just take one and leave the other for later, eh?"

Before I knew what was happening, he did the following: rammed the bottle back in the box. Slammed the lid on it. Lunged at Amelia. Jammed her under one arm and the box under the other. And then they all vanished—Mordo, Amelia, the box, and the bottle with the tiny boat still inside it.

I felt a cold draft of air, but that was about all. Where they had been, there was nothing at all. It was as if a huge soap bubble had burst right in front of me. Except that a soap bubble would have left a little damp spot as a reminder that it had been there. But there was no damp spot now. No spot at all. Nothing!

4

Puzzles and Problems

For several moments, I just stood in a dumb stupor, staring at the place where Mordo and Amelia had been. It was as if I were watching a television screen that had suddenly gone blank, and was waiting for the announcer's voice to tell me everything was all right, and the picture would be right back. But it finally sank in that the magic of Mordo had nothing to do with the magic of television, and they were gone. G-o-n-e, as in vanished! My legs turned to jelly under me, and I thumped down onto the side of my bed.

Mordo had said something about taking us back to his century. *Which* century? And even if I knew, how would I get there; by plane? Ha! Ha! Me and my dumb saxophone, I thought. If I hadn't been waving that around, Amelia and I would be together right then. But possibly as toads, and what good would I be to either of us, in that condition? No, it was probably better that I was where I was, and still in the old, familiar shape of Rupert P. Brown III. But what could I do even in *that* shape? *What?*

"Rupert! Amelia!" My mother's voice, wafting up the stairs, alerted me to the fact that she was on her way to my room.

What was I going to tell her when she discovered Amelia was no longer with us? That a little man had jumped out of a bottle and vanished with her? I was faced with the same old problem. Tell the truth, in accord with my truthful, accurate, scientific nature, and I'd be rushed to the doctor, or at least into bed with a cold compress on my head. I thought fast. Then I quickly unlocked the door, dove in and out of the closet, and was halfway into my purple-striped flannel pajamas when my mother arrived.

"How nice, dear, that you're already getting into your pajamas!" She looked relieved that we were not going to have our usual argument about it. "I gather Amelia has already gone to bed."

That was exactly what I hoped my mother would gather. I didn't say anything but appeared to concentrate on buttoning my pajama top. I hoped my fingers weren't shaking too much. "Oh my, I hope I didn't wake Amelia up calling up the stairs," my mother said.

"She—she's probably too far gone," I replied. Truthfully.

"Well, dear—" My mother kissed me goodnight. "See you in the morning!"

Morning! That was another problem. What was I going to do about Amelia in the morning? I finished climbing into my pajamas, and went over to talk to my three pets: Caruso, my turtle, and Hector and Guinevere, my two guinea pigs. If only they could talk to *me* the way they did when I had entered the agreement to help Miss Switch. Now, all I could do was talk to *them*.

"I know you couldn't do anything about bringing Amelia back," I said. "But if you could just talk again, maybe you could give me some ideas about helping her, the way you did when I had to help Miss Switch. Without you, and without Miss Switch, I'm all alone in this thing." I gave a deep sigh, and shook my head sadly. "Well, good-night, everybody!"

They blinked their bright little beady, intelligent eyes at me, but I couldn't be certain that they had understood one word I'd said. In despair, I headed for my desk, en route to bed. There I pulled open the drawer marked "Private—Keep Out—This Means You!" and took out a small notebook I hadn't used in a long, long time. On the first page I had written, "Miss Switch—Notes." The first note was as follows:

34

What:	Eyes
Kind:	Crackling
Whose:	Hers
Performance:	Sees clearly from back of head
How Tested:	No known way to prove scientifically

I read through all the other notes, most of them similar to this one. When I had finished reading, I hesitated, and then picked up my pencil stub and turned to a fresh page. With trembling hand, I wrote the words, "Mordo— Notes." Underneath, I wrote the following:

What:	Warlock
Kind:	The worst
Whose:	Ugly-nosed Witch's (probably)
Performance:	Emerged from bottle in shape of one-inch sea captain. Transformed self into six-foot-six warlock. Vanished with Amelia.
How Tested:	No known way to prove scientifically

I studied these new notes for some time, but found nothing there of much use. I finally put them away, and fell wearily into my bed. There, more frightening thoughts went racing through my mind, keeping me tossing and turning for a long time. Then I finally fell into a restless sleep.

At about midnight I was awakened suddenly by the strange sound of someone singing right inside my room. Had I left on my new antique shortwave radio, which rarely worked, but might have finally decided to honor me in the middle of the night with a song? Or was this another nifty little surprise from the witch? I lay stiff and frozen in my bed, listening.

"O sole mio! O dum-dee-deeo!"

"Oh, do be still, Caruso!" a stern voice interrupted. "You're going to wake Rupert up. After all he's been through, the poor dear needs his sleep."

Caruso, of course! "O Sole Mio" was his favorite song. I should have guessed. And that was Guinevere's voice, sounding just like a miniature version of my mother. I should have recognized that, too. I hurled myself out of bed, switched on the light, and tore over to their cages.

"You're—you're talking again!" I gasped.

"I thought I was singing!" Caruso replied huffily.

"I'm sorry," I said. I'd forgotten that you had to be pretty careful about Caruso and his voice. He was very touchy on the subject.

"Oh, for goodness sake, Caruso," Guine-

36

vere said. "Don't be such a prima donna. This is a very exciting event, our being able to talk with Rupert again."

"Of course it is!" agreed Hector. "It's not nearly so much fun just talking amongst ourselves."

"That's right," said Caruso. "It's pretty boring when all anyone wants to discuss is guinea-pig feed."

"Well," said Hector with a sniff, "it's also pretty boring when all anyone *else* wants to discuss is whether he's in voice."

"Boys! Boys!" Guinevere scolded. "Some terrible things happened to Rupert tonight, and I'm certain he wants to talk them over with us."

"Wow, do I ever!" I cried. I quickly dragged my desk chair over close to my pets, and collapsed into it. "I guess you must have seen everything that went on in my room."

"You bet we did!" said Hector.

"And it was terrible!" exclaimed Guinevere.

Caruso hoisted himself up onto the side of his bowl and blinked his pebbly green eyes at me. "We were all scared to death, Rupert. I personally withdrew into my shell and stayed there for the duration. I would have invited poor Hector and Guinevere to join me, but there's only room for one in here, you know."

"I do know," I said. "And I'm *sure* you would have invited them in if you could."

37

"So are we!" Hector and Guinevere chorused wholeheartedly.

This was true. Hector and Guinevere and Caruso might snipe at each other about guinea-pig feed and Caruso's singing, but underneath it all, they were very close friends. Overcome with emotion, Caruso lost his balance and toppled over on his back, where he lay flailing his legs helplessly. I quickly turned him right-side-up again.

"Thank you, Rupert! You don't know how much I appreciate it when you do that." Caruso had a catch in his throat. "And—and I'd like to say now that I'm sorry I woke you up. I didn't know if I had a voice left after all the scares, and I'm afraid I just wanted to try it out."

"That's all right, Caruso, I understand," I told him. "There were a few times tonight when I thought I'd lost my voice myself. But speaking of voices, what do you suppose has happened that's making you able to talk to me again?"

My pets all looked at one another and shrugged.

Then Guinevere twitched her whiskers thoughtfully. "When we were able to talk to you before, Rupert, it was because you had entered into an agreement with a witch. Isn't a warlock a male witch?"

"Of course he is!" Caruso broke in. "Good thinking, Guinevere."

"But I didn't make any agreement with him," I said.

"You certainly didn't!" exclaimed Hector. "At least I didn't hear you agreeing to let him turn you and Amelia into toads."

"I'm sorry, Rupert. I wasn't thinking," said Guinevere. "That big bully!" she added furiously.

"How about the witch who gave you the bottle?" Caruso asked. "Did you by any chance enter into some kind of agreement with her?"

I thought a moment. "The only thing I can think of is that she scared me into saying I wouldn't tell anyone about her so-called present."

"Well, there you are!" said Caruso triumphantly.

"There you are, nothing," said Hector. "If a witch threatened you like that, Caruso, what would *you* do?"

"Agree to anything, just like Rupert. Which makes it an agreement, doesn't it?"

Guinevere sighed. "That's pretty flimsy, Caruso. But it does seem to be the best answer we have at the moment."

"I guess it really doesn't matter, anyway," I said. "What really matters is rescuing Amelia. I don't know *where* she is, or *when* she is, or even *what* she is. She might already be a toad, for all I know. And what am I going to do about it?" I groaned.

39

"What about science?" Caruso asked.

"Couldn't you put your fertile brain to work on some travel-back-in-time pills, or some anti-toad potion?"

"I'm only a great scientist, Caruso, not a great sorcerer. I wouldn't know where to begin on that other kind of stuff."

"How about some of those interesting things Miss Switch used, like wing of bat and eye of newt and stool of toad," suggested Hector.

"That's *toadstool*," I corrected him. "But none of those things would do much good. Miss Switch used them, only she didn't really believe in them. She said they were old-fashioned."

"Well, you have to start somewhere," Caruso said. "And those things are as good a place to start as any."

I shook my head. "I'm afraid there's only one ingredient that could do any good in my life right now—Miss Switch!"

Guinevere hesitated. "Maybe—maybe she's the one, Rupert."

"The one what?"

"The one who's the reason we're able to talk to you again."

"She couldn't be," I said. "My agreement with her ended when we put the Comput-o-witch out of business, and Saturna got banished from Witch's Mountain."

"Maybe," Caruso broke in. "But maybe once you have a pact with a witch, you always have one. That may be one of the rules and regulations pertaining to witchcraft that we don't know about.''

"Miss Switch might just turn up at school tomorrow," Hector said.

I sighed deeply. "Maybe, Hector, but I doubt it."

"Well, in the meantime, Rupert, I suggest you get right back to bed, and try to get some sleep," Guinevere said firmly. "Whether Miss Switch is back or not, you're going to need all your wits about you tomorrow."

"I know. And there's another thing." I sighed again. "What am I going to tell my mother and father about Amelia tomorrow?"

Caruso, Guinevere, and Hector all looked at one another in dismay. They knew how far I would get if I told my parents exactly what happened.

"It looks as if you're going to have to resort to the old fertile brain to make up a tale," Caruso advised me.

"We know it's very tough on a scientist like you, devoted to truth and accuracy," Hector said. "But what else can you do?"

"Not much. And even making up a tale isn't all that easy."

"Poor thing!" crooned Guinevere. "Perhaps when you've had a good night's sleep, something will come to you."

"I hope so. Anyway, I guess I'd better turn

in now. Goodnight, all of you. And—and thanks!"

"Goodnight, Rupert!" my pets all chorused sympathetically.

"By the way, Rupert—" Caruso hesitated. "You—you wouldn't like a little lullaby to help you get to sleep, would you?"

"Sure, Caruso!" I couldn't help a weak grin as I flicked out my light and crawled into bed. But I have to confess it was certainly good to hear that thin, little voice piping the familiar "Brahms' Lullaby" across the room. It reminded me that, whatever happened, I wasn't all alone now, facing the problem of Mordo and the terrible disaster that had befallen Amelia.

5

Kidnapped

By morning, my fertile brain had not suggested a single helpful hint on how to explain the disappearance of a friend from our house in the middle of the night. I dawdled around getting dressed as long as I possibly could. I brushed my teeth slowly and carefully *twice,* and even scrubbed my ears, which I rarely do except on holidays and the last day of school. But I finally ran out of things to keep myself busy upstairs, so I had to appear at the breakfast table.

"Goodness, where's Amelia?" my mother asked at once. "She's usually up and downstairs long before you, dear."

I breathed an inward sigh of relief that this was at least one question I could answer without any trouble. "I don't know," I said, which was the whole and simple truth. I then plopped down at the table and overstuffed my mouth with a tablespoonful of the cinnamon oatmeal my mother had set down in front of me. I hoped this little distraction might take everyone's mind off the subject of Amelia, so I would have more time to think. But it didn't work.

"Oh dear!" said my mother after a few moments. "Where *is* that child? It's not like her to dawdle. Her oatmeal is going to get cold."

My father set down his coffee cup and appeared at once from behind the newspaper.

"Rupert, why don't you help your mother by running upstairs and getting Amelia."

I could have given my father a very good reason why it was a waste of time for me to do that, but I didn't. I just climbed the stairs anyway, and checked out Amelia's room, and then the bathroom. For good measure, I even checked out the linen closet. Then I returned downstairs to make my report. "She's not there," I said, which was still the absolute truth.

"What do you mean, 'not there'?" asked my father.

"I mean, I couldn't find her," I replied. So far, so good.

"Rupert," my father said sternly, "you're not trying to be funny, are you?"

"No." If my father could have heard my heart thumping in my chest just then, he would have known exactly how funny I was *not* trying to be.

"Well, I'm going to go see for myself," said my mother.

"So am I," said my father. "And you had better be right, Rupert," he added sternly.

I was certain that this was not what my father meant to say, but I decided against making a smart remark about it. I sat there listening to their steps go thumping up the stairs, and then a few minutes later, come thumping down again. They returned to the kitchen.

"Amelia really isn't there," said my mother. She looked pale.

"That's what I said," I said.

"She must be *someplace* around the house," my father said briskly.

My mother brightened at this thought. "Why yes! She's probably off in a corner somewhere, with her nose buried in one of Rupert's science books."

"Well, what are we waiting for?" asked my father. "Let's all go look for her."

"Amelia! Amelia! Amelia!" we all shouted as we spread out through the house. I looked just as hard as anyone, peering under chairs, lifting up the magazines on the coffee table, looking behind pictures on the walls.

"Don't be ridiculous, Rupert," said my father.

"Well, you never know," I said, which was entirely the truth.

Naturally, as you might suspect, we did not find Amelia. We all returned empty-handed to the kitchen. By now, my father was also beginning to look pale.

"When did you last see Amelia?" he asked me.

"In my room."

"She—she didn't say anything about being unhappy over something and—and wanting to run away, did she?" my mother asked.

"Not a word."

"Well, she couldn't have just vanished," said my father firmly. *"That's* impossible."

Needless to say, I refrained from expressing any opinion about this. "Maybe she was kidnapped," I suggested brightly. I thought this was pretty brilliant on my part, because while still sticking to my principles of truth and accuracy, I was also giving my parents a really helpful suggestion to put their minds to rest.

What happened was that my mother and father looked as if a steel ball had fallen on their respective heads. *"KIDNAPPED!"* they cried. I felt terrible then, of course, although I suspect that after a while they would have had this idea on their own.

"Kidnapped from under our very own roof!" moaned my mother. "How could it have happened?"

I let my father have this question.

"Now, let's not panic," said my father bravely. "The first thing I'm going to do is go to the Daleys' house to see if Amelia might not have run home for something. Rupert, you'd better go on to school. Don't say anything to anybody about this just yet, but keep your ears open, especially during roll call. Someone might have something to say about Amelia. Then telephone us at once with whatever news you have. If she's not at her home, and there's no word of her whereabouts, then I guess we'll have to—to call the police."

"The police!" My mother collapsed into the nearest chair. "Oh my goodness me!"

6

Back in Charge

"Yah! Yah! Yah!" An unpleasant voice broke into my worried thoughts as I entered the playground. It was the voice of Melvin Bothwick, Pepperdine fifth grade's worst sneak. "Where's your girl friend, Amelia?" sneered Melvin.

"Wouldn't you like to know!" I said. I couldn't help wishing someone would turn *Melvin* into a toad. The only problem was that probably his friends and his family wouldn't even notice the difference.

My friends Wayne Partlow (alias Peatmouse), Harvey Fanna (alias Banana), and Tommy Conrad (alias Creampuff) all heard what was going on, and came running over to protect me from Melvin. A cloak of secrecy (an expression left over from the days when I was a great detective) was supposed to descend on the information about Amelia staying at my house for a week, but somehow the news had

leaked out. My friends were all very nice about
it. They worried that two great scientists getting
together might blow up our house, but nobody
teased us or anything. Just Melvin. Also Billy
Swanson, the Pepperdine fifth grade's big bully.

"Broomstick, where *is* Amelia?" Peatmouse
asked. He wasn't being nosy like Melvin; just
asking. (Broomstick, as you may have guessed,
is *my* alias. This is because I am very skinny.
It is an interesting nickname, though, when you
consider that it was given to me long before
certain recent events in my life.)

"She's not here," I answered Peatmouse.

"Oh," said Peatmouse. "Hey, look, the
monkey bars are empty! Let's go sit on top
until the bell rings."

That's the way friends are. Nobody asks a
lot of nosy questions. To tell the truth, though,
I didn't want to go sit on the monkey bars just
then. I wanted to go sit at my desk and see if
Miss Switch was there. But no one in their right
mind, unless they're a super genius, or it's
ninety below zero outside, rushes into their
classroom before the bell rings. So I went and
sat on top of the monkey bars.

When I finally went pushing and shoving
(which is our usual manner of entry) into the
classroom with my friends, I decided I might
just as well have perched on top of those monkey bars until I grew tail feathers, or my ears
froze off, whichever came first. There was no

Miss Switch sitting, or standing, behind the Pepperdine Elementary School fifth-grade teacher's desk. It was just ordinary, medium-old, fuzzy-red-haired Mrs. Fitzgerald, who had been there the day before, and the day before that. All hope gone, I plunked down at my desk in despair.

The final bell rang, and Mrs. Fitzgerald began the roll call. "Archibald, Robert."

"Present," said Archibald, Robert.

I kept my ears open, as requested by my father, while we went through Anderson, Liza; Bothwick, Melvin; Brown, Rupert; and Conrad, Tommy.

"Daley, Amelia," said Mrs. Fitzgerald.

I surveyed the room intently, but nobody looked as if they had even heard of Daley, Amelia.

"Daley, Amelia," repeated Mrs. Fitzgerald. "Absent." She checked the absent place in her book.

Bothwick, Melvin, immediately directed a sneaky sneer in my direction. *"Rupert* knows where Amelia is!"

"Oh," said Mrs. Fitzgerald, "is Amelia someplace she isn't supposed to be?"

This was a loaded question. I had to think a moment. "She—she's not well," I said, which was the truth as far as I was concerned. How else could you describe a possible case of toad-itis? Fortunately, Mrs. Fitzgerald didn't ask any more questions, but I threw Bothwick, Melvin, a dark look as she went on with the roll call.

The only other thing that happened was Billy Swanson showing off by saying "present, present, present," like a broken record. He didn't stop until Mrs. Fitzgerald threatened to send him to the principal. Boy, I thought sadly, he wouldn't have dared pull one of his tricks like that one on Miss Switch!

As soon as all the names had been called, I got myself excused to make my report home that Amelia was not present or heard from. It was not a very cheerful telephone call.

"Oh dear!" said my mother in a fading voice. "I guess we *will* have to call the police and—and Amelia's parents." I felt sorry for my mother and father, but I didn't know who had it worse, them, or me. After all, it was my narrow, not-quite-eleven-year-old shoulders on which rested the whole fate of Daley, Amelia.

I managed to drag myself through ordinary, medium-old, fuzzy-red-haired Mrs. Fitzgerald's morning exercises, which unfortunately my telephone call did not help me to miss, and lend my squeaky voice to the morning song. Today it was "Twinkle, Twinkle, Little Star," which is a very dippy number for fifth grade, but happens to be one of Mrs. Fitzgerald's favorites. At any rate, it did at least seem to fit the

51

occasion. I mean, when you think about the "wonder what you are" part.

All that over, I sank into my desk to think. Science was now definitely the only thing left to me. While classroom business was being conducted, I devoted half my mind to reviewing all the chemical powders and liquids I had in my collection at home. But the other half was devoted to hollering, "What should I do, Miss Switch? *HELP!*" And this, of course, left no part of my mind to pay attention to the English lesson, the arithmetic lesson, or Mrs. Fitzgerald being called away for a telephone call. I only managed a faint sigh of resignation as the usual thing happened whenever she left the room.

Melvin looked around for someone to sneer at, and Billy Swanson looked around for some kind of mischief to get into. It didn't take either of them long. Melvin settled on me. His lips drew back over his teeth into a kind of leer. "Yah! Yah! Yah! Rupert's stuck on Amelia. Yah! Yah! Yah!"

In the meantime, Billy found what he was looking for, too. He stumped up to the front of the classroom, picked up two blackboard erasers, and began banging them together. Clouds of chalk dust flew out into the room, and into everyone's noses and lungs. Cough! Cough! Cough! went the class.

"Cut it out, Billy!" someone yelled at him.

But Billy went right on banging the erasers with a big grin on his face. "Try and make me!"

"All right, if that's what you want, then that's exactly what I'll do!" said a commanding voice from the doorway.

Then, instantly, all the chalk dust gathered itself up from all over the classroom into one big white cloud, which went swooshing right back to Billy. The cloud swirled around him like a tornado.

Cough! Cough! "Help! Help! I'm choking to death!" yelled Billy.

"Are you ready to start behaving yourself?" asked the voice from the doorway.

"I'm ready! I'm ready! I've already started!" hollered Billy, dancing around inside the cloud of chalk dust, clutching his throat.

"Very well then!" returned the voice. And with that, all the chalk dust suddenly swooshed right back up into the erasers. Billy was so startled that he let go of them, and they fell clattering to the floor.

"Now," he was told, "you may lean over, pick up the erasers, put them back on the blackboard, and return yourself to your seat!"

As the pink-eared Billy leaned, picked, put, and returned, the hypnotized class now turned its attention to the person who had performed this remarkable feat. Then everyone, including me, gave one great big gasp. *"MISS SWITCH!"*

There she was, in that same ancient gray
dress with the high collar edged in a white
ruffle, black hair pulled back into a plain old
bun, and on her sharp, pinched nose those same
metal-framed spectacles that perched there like
a grasshopper. As comfortable-looking as a
steel knitting needle; that's what she was like
before, and that's what she was like now. You
would hardly expect this to be someone a class
would go wild about seeing again. But there
you are, and it only goes to prove, looks sure
aren't everything!

Miss Switch came striding right into the
classroom and up to the teacher's desk as if she
had never been away. I knew her well enough
to know how pleased she probably was that the
class was so pleased to have her back, but you
sure wouldn't have known it from the stern,
no-more-nonsense-now look she gave everyone. She stood at the desk with those crackling,
snapping eyes that could hush up a whispering
class in an instant.

"Mrs. Fitzgerald has been called away on a
sudden emergency," she said. "I am here today as your substitute teacher. I believe all of
you remember who I am, but to refresh the
memories of those who might not, I shall again
write my name on the blackboard." Then, just
as she had done before, she wrote the following
in the same big swooping letters:

MISS SWITCH

"Has anyone anything they would like to say before we begin our lessons?" she asked in a voice that left no doubt she really did not expect anybody to do that.

But somebody did, anyway.

"Heelp! Heelp!" squeaked a voice that sounded as if it were being forced through the teeth of a comb. "Mee meeooth ees steeuck. Eee ceen't cleeoose me leeps."

"Of course you can't, Melvin Bothwick," said Miss Switch briskly. "I told you before, that one of these days your mouth would be fixed in a permanent sneer. Now, do you seriously wish to do something about it?"

"Yees! Yees!" squealed Melvin desperately.

"Then please write, 'I will never sneer at anyone again' one hundred times, starting now. When you've finished, I'm sure you will be feeling much better."

I'll bet the "Guinness Book of Records" has never recorded anyone diving for pencil and paper and starting to write as fast as Melvin!

Good old Miss Switch was back in charge again! I exchanged grins with Peatmouse, Banana, and Creampuff. You have to remember, though, as I noted earlier, that only Amelia and I knew about Miss Switch being a witch, a real one. The rest of Pepperdine's fifth grade only

knew her as a terrific teacher. A few people might have had some suspicions about the witch part, but they never pursued the subject. So in the end, it was only I, Rupert P. Brown III, in my quest for scientific truth, and Amelia M. Daley, snooping along behind me, who had made the discovery.

Amelia! Omigosh! In my joy at seeing Miss Switch again, and all that stuff going on with Billy and Melvin, I almost forgot my basic, most important reason for wanting her back again. Now she *was* back, but what was to say she had returned to help me rescue Amelia? I squirmed around in my desk, hoping she would tell me I was a disturbing influence, or something like that, and invite me to stay after school. Then I would know that *she* knew. But though I squirmed and squirmed, and sent frantic glances in her direction, she paid no attention to me at all. I finally gave up, and stared down at my desk in despair.

"Rupert!"

I nearly shot right up out of my desk like a rocket. "Y-y-yes, M-M-Miss Switch?"

"I had hoped that when I returned to this class, I just might see some improvement in your miserable penmanship. Chicken scratches! Hmmmph!" snorted Miss Switch. "As soon as the recess bell rings, please come to my desk, and we shall have a discussion about this."

"Yes, Miss Switch." I concentrated on looking as unhappy as possible before the sympathetic glances of my fifth-grade class. But it was all I could do to keep my face glued into a worried expression until the bell clanged for recess.

As soon as the last member of the class left, who happened to be Peatmouse (because he had stayed behind to drop a few words of courage into my ear), I flew up to the teacher's desk.

"Miss Switch, you're back!"

"Of course I am!" snapped Miss Switch. "You didn't think I'd let you or Amelia down, did you?"

"But—but you said you weren't ever coming back. I mean, except as a cloud passing by. We just about gave up wishing."

"Well, for your information, Rupert, I received all those earlier mental messages from the two of you, but I'm not a fairy godmother who runs around granting every little whim and fancy." Sparks shot out from Miss Switch's eyes and danced on the desk.

I edged back a half inch. After all, even though I knew how much Miss Switch liked Amelia and me and the Pepperdine fifth grade, a witch was still a witch, and I'm one who does not believe in taking unnecessary risks.

"So—so what made you decide to come now, Miss Switch?"

"Some very powerful vibrations from both you and Amelia, Rupert. Very powerful, indeed! I recognized that these were not your usual little wishy-washy-wish-you-were-here wishes. I came then as soon as I could. Arrangements had to be made, of course. You don't just walk into Pepperdine Elementary School and announce you're going to take over the fifth grade, you know."

"I guess not," I said.

Miss Switch's glance suddenly drifted away from me down to somebody's English paper on her desk. "Tsk! Tsk!" She made several slashing red marks on it. "Very sloppy work!" She seemed to have forgotten all about me. I cleared my throat delicately, causing her to glare at me. "Well?"

"W-w-well what?" I stammered, wondering what I had done wrong. After all, it wasn't my English paper she was murdering.

"Well, where is Amelia, of course!"

"Oh! She—she's vanished, Miss Switch."

"What do you mean 'vanished'? Did she just wander out of her house? You children must learn to be more specific."

"I mean *vanished* vanished, Miss Switch. She was standing beside me in my room with Mordo, and the next moment they weren't. Gone, phffft, just like that! They were about as vanished as you can get."

"Mordo?" inquired Miss Switch. "Do you, by any chance, mean Mordo the warlock?"

"By any chance I sure do!" I exclaimed. "Do you know him, Miss Switch?"

"Not well, Rupert. Actually, he was active somewhat before my time, a century or two ago, but he hasn't been heard from for some while. I understand that something happened to him, although I can't remember what. He wasn't much of a warlock, either. Quite second-rate, I believe. Had only one trick he specialized in, but I can't remember that either."

"He was pretty scary, Miss Switch," I said.

Miss Switch sniffed. "When you're talking witches, scary doesn't mean a thing. We're all scary, one way or another. But at least there's no question that witchcraft is involved here. Hmmm!" She rubbed her pointed chin thoughtfully. "No wonder the thought vibrations were so strong. Well, go on, go on! Don't just stand there, Rupert. Tell me what led up to this vanishment."

"May I sit down, Miss Switch?" I asked. This was going to be a long story, probably taking up all the rest of recess.

"Be my guest!"

I dropped into the nearest desk, which happened to be Billy Swanson's, pushed aside Billy's debris, propped my elbows on the desk top, and launched into my story.

I began by explaining how Amelia was staying at our house, and how a strange witch had arrived on the doorstep the night before, with a present for Amelia and me.

"Did she say who she was, this witch?" asked Miss Switch sharply.

"No, but she had the worst-looking nose I've ever seen in my life. Like a big hunk of moldy green cheese."

"Hmmm!" mused Miss Switch. "Could be any one of a number of witches I know, but my guess would be Gulldemonia. She has a nose that would stop a clock. The question is, what is she up to? Tell me, Rupert, what *was* the present?"

I told Miss Switch about the nifty, shipshape, shining little ship floating inside a bottle, and how Amelia and I had heated the bottle over my alcohol lamp and popped out the cork, along with one-inch-tall Captain Mordecai. "Boy, was he furious with us for practically wrecking his boots. I guess he really loved those boots! Anyway, he started to get bigger and bigger. When he got so big he practically filled my room, he suddenly turned into Mordo, the warlock. Well, after that—"

"Aha!" shouted Miss Switch. "Now it all comes back to me. Sometime during his century, whenever it was, he was doing a lot of things that were giving witches such a bad name, a lot of perfectly harmless—well, *almost* perfectly harmless—witches were being hounded to death and punished for absolutely nothing—

well, *almost* absolutely nothing. So some good—well, *reasonably* good—witch got fed up with it all, and lured him into the bottle, using that little ship as bait. She cast a spell on it so that it could only be opened in one particular way, which you and Amelia hit upon, Rupert.''

"Gosh!" I said.

"Yes, Rupert! So proud of his one-and-only noteworthy trick he was, that he ran it to the ground. The memory of that has come back to me, too. It was turning people into toads, willy nilly, with no selectivity whatsoever. No wonder that—''

"Toad! Toad!" I burst in excitedly. "That's exactly what he was trying to do to *us;* turn us into toads, Miss Switch. He couldn't do it, though, so he said he was going to take us back to his century, whatever that was. That was when I grabbed my saxophone and scared him off with it. You know the kind of notes I blow on it, Miss Switch.''

"I know!" she said agreeably. "Good thinking, Rupert!"

"Well, sort of good thinking," I said. "It scared Mordo off me, but before I knew what was happening, he grabbed Amelia, and that's when they vanished. What are we going to do, Miss Switch? We've got to get Amelia back right away. My mother and father don't know about Mordo, but they do know Amelia's missing. They think she's just plain kidnapped, and that's bad enough. They're going to call the police and Amelia's parents. It's awful!''

"Blast and botheration!" said Miss Switch. "I'd forgotten that mothers and fathers would be involved with this. That *is* awful, Rupert, but not much we can do about it today, not without causing even deeper problems. I'm afraid you'll have to return here tonight at the witching hour."

"The witching hour?" I asked blankly.

"Oh, for goodness sake, Rupert!" Several more sparks danced on the desk in front of me. "Twelve o'clock midnight! I thought you were up on these things by now."

"I'm sorry, Miss Switch. I guess I've got too much on my mind. But golly, I sure wish we didn't have to wait until then. Amelia might already be turned into a—a—" I couldn't say the word.

"I know what you mean, Rupert, but it's a chance we have to take. We'll have to count on Mordo being his usual second-rate self, that's all."

"Anyway," I said, "I don't know what I would have done without you, Miss Switch. Thanks for coming back!" To my embarrassment, my voice came out a little thick and funny sounding.

"Now, let's not have any sentimental nonsense, Rupert. You know how I feel about that sort of thing." Miss Switch suddenly looked down and began shuffling some papers around on her desk. Her voice sounded a little funny, too.

By then, however, the end-of-recess bell had rung, and Peatmouse, Banana, Creampuff, and the rest of the fifth grade came trooping back into the room.

"Please return to your seat, Rupert!" Miss Switch sounded like Miss Switch again. "I do hope this little lesson in penmanship has not been a total waste of time. Remember to work on your p's and q's. *Twelve hours* of practice should do it." Her eyebrows slithered meaningfully up her forehead, and I got the message. Twelve o'clock that night!

It was going to be a long wait. Miss Switch might think Mordo was second-rate, but that whole vanishing act didn't look too second-rate to me. Well, at least it was no longer just me and a couple of powders and liquids off my science lab table against witchcraft. It was going to be witchcraft versus witchcraft. Miss Switch versus Mordo!

But why didn't I feel reassured about this? Why did it sound so scary? Well, I finally concluded, that's because I, Rupert P. Brown III, was still right in the middle of the whole thing. With a shudder, I picked up my well-chewed yellow pencil, and began a row of wobbly p's and q's.

7

Detective Plume

When I arrived home that afternoon after school, there was a strange black car parked in front of our house. There was also a strange dark-haired man in our living room with my mother and father. He was making notes in a small black notebook when I appeared.

"Rupert, this is Detective Plume," said my mother, who looked as if she hadn't recovered yet from the iron ball falling on her head that morning. So did my father, for that matter.

"Detective Plume wants to ask you some questions," my father said.

Me being interrogated (which, as you probably know, is detectivese for *questioned*) by a real-live, honest-to-gosh detective! If this had been back in my great-detective period, I would have been jumping out of my skin. Unfortunately, it wasn't. Also unfortunately, Detective Plume was short and plump, with bright pink cheeks. And there wasn't enough of the dark hair even to cover the top of his head. He was not exactly my idea of how a great detective ought to look. But I couldn't help that, so I just plunked myself down on the nearest chair and got ready to be interrogated.

Detective Plume cleared his plump throat and gave me an encouraging smile. "Now, Rupert, it seems that you were the last person to have seen Amelia. Can you remember exactly what happened before she left the room?"

Oh-oh, here we go again! I thought. But, as always, I was determined to be as truthful as possible. I thought farther. "We were having a conversation," I said.

"Having a conversation," repeated Detective Plume, while writing this down in his notebook. "What was the conversation about?"

"An experiment we had just done. It had to do with expansion of steam. We had a corked bottle with some water in it. We brought the water to a boil over my alcohol burner, and out popped the cork."

"Expansion of steam. Out popped cork," wrote Detective Plume busily in his notebook.

"We're afraid some day Rupert might blow up the house," said my father, by way of a joke to liven up the occasion.

"Might blow up house," wrote Detective Plume. He must not have thought this as funny as my father usually does, because when he

66

looked up at me again, he attempted a steely-eyed, piercing look. I know about this because, during my great-detective period, I used to practice it on myself in the bathroom mirror.

"And I believe your mother said that after that, Amelia went to bed?" he asked.

"That's right," I replied, which was the absolute truth. That *was* what my mother said.

Detective Plume fixed me with another piercing stare. "And you didn't see Amelia again that evening?"

"Not once."

"She didn't say anything about running away, or going to visit a friend?"

"Not a word."

"Hmmm!" hummed Detective Plume, tapping his pencil on his notebook. "This certainly is a very puzzling case. Are you quite certain you're telling me everything you know, Rupert?" The look he gave me this time practically impaled me to the living room wall.

"Y-yes," I said, unfortunately hesitating a moment too long.

Detective Plume pounced. "Aha! This boy has not been telling the truth!"

Then I lost my head. "No," I blurted, "I'm not! What really happened is that this warlock jumped out of the bottle along with the cork, and vanished with Amelia!"

"Oh dear!" moaned my mother. "The strain has been too much for him."

67

"You had better go up to your room and rest, Rupert," said my father.

"Strain too much," Detective Plume scribbled in his notebook.

Well, no one could say I hadn't tried. I only wished I could tell my poor, scared mother and father that there was someone who really might help find Amelia, someone at present sitting in Pepperdine Elementary School's fifth-grade classroom, busily correcting arithmetic papers, and not interrogating anybody.

But there was nothing more I could say, so I retreated to my room, as ordered. There, I could make my report to the only ones in the whole house who would listen to the truth and actually believe it, and that just happened to be a turtle and two guinea pigs. Which is pretty strange, if you stop to think about it.

8

Blackboard Bewitched

Caruso had to sing three lullabyes that night to put me to sleep. Actually, I think he put himself to sleep first, because it was awfully quiet in my room long before my eyes finally drifted shut. Then it seemed as if I had only just fallen asleep when the alarm clock hidden under my pillow awakened me with its rude buzz.

If you've read my earlier account, you would know that by now I am an old hand at these middle-of-the-night adventures. But it never seems to get any easier. With the world dark and silent around me, I jumped out of bed, getting goose bumps over goose bumps as I shoved myself into my chilly underwear and trousers. Then, after thrusting my icy toes into my icy socks and sneakers, I picked up the flashlight I always keep on my desk for emergencies, and shone it on my pets to make sure they were all right before I took off. After all, who knew how long it was going to be before I got back.

Hector and Caruso were snoring gently away, sound asleep, but Guinevere looked back at me with bright, wide-awake eyes.

"How come you're awake?" I asked.

"Well, *someone* had to see to it that you got up and were safely on your way." Guinevere shook her head despairingly at Hector and Caruso. "Good thing I didn't count on them. Have you got your earmuffs, Rupert?"

"Heck, I don't need earmuffs, Guinevere."

"Rupert, you take your earmuffs!" said Guinevere sternly. "You just might be very glad to have them."

"Oh, okay," I grumbled. "I'll get them when I pick up my jacket in the coat closet. Any other instructions?"

"Have you got the toadstools?"

"What toadstools?"

"Why, the ones you gathered for Miss Switch when she bewitched the Pepperdine football game. Goodness, Rupert, I'm surprised at your forgetting. You still have some left, don't you?"

"Oh sure!" I said, although to be honest, I *had* just about forgotten about them. After all, none of my scientific experiments called for toadstools. I couldn't even remember where they were. "But Miss Switch didn't ask for them. She doesn't believe much in that kind of stuff."

"Take them!" said Guinevere. "You never

know when something like that might come in handy. Third shelf, second bottle from the left, Rupert.''

There were only two toadstools in the bottle, so I took them both and stuck them in my pants pocket. ''May I go now?'' I shone the flashlight again on Guinevere. To my surprise, I saw a teardrop glistening on her nose. ''Look, you don't have to worry. If anything happens, my mother and father will take care of you all.''

''Goose!'' exclaimed Guinevere. *''We're* not who I'm worried about. It's *you.''*

''I'll be okay. Don't you worry, Guinevere!'' I reached into her cage, patted her on the head, and then left the room with chin up and shoulders back. Rupert P. Brown III, scientist, adventurer, dabbler in witchcraft!

Also, Rupert P. Brown III, scared to death! When I finally arrived at the Pepperdine Elementary School playground, I reached another conclusion. It was never going to get any easier seeing a plain old red-brick building, that looked so ordinary in the daylight, suddenly turn into a big, hulking shadow, with the moonlight turning its windows into glistening, evil-looking eyes. I could hear my heart thumping in my ears as I raced across the blacktop to the ground-floor window that would let me into my fifth-grade classroom. A small light glowed through the window from inside the room— probably the Bunsen burner, I told myself, if

I remembered correctly. And in front of that Bunsen burner would be my teacher.

No, not the teacher in the gray dress with the ruffled collar, her hair in a strict bun, and funny little glasses perched on her nose. It would be my teacher wearing a tall, pointed black hat, which cast weird shadows on the blackboard, a black cape, and no little glasses hiding her slanted, glass-green eyes that sent out sparks as crackling as a Fourth-of-July firecracker. And on her teacher's desk, carelessly flicking a long, pointed tail over a stack of fifth-grade test papers, would be a huge black cat with eyes as slanted and glass-green as her owner's. For this would now be Miss Switch the Witch in my fifth-grade classroom, and her cat Bathsheba!

But even with all this advance knowledge, as I shoved open the window and threw my legs over the windowsill, I felt as if I were turning into one big ice cube when I actually saw what my mind had been telling me all along that I would see.

"H-h-hello, Miss Switch!"

But Miss Switch acted as if I had never even arrived. In the dim light of the Bunsen burner, I noted that her eyes were fixed on something lying on her desk. As far as I could tell, it looked like nothing more than a plain old blackboard eraser, like the kind employed earlier in the day by Billy Swanson.

I moved closer to her desk. "I—I'm here, Miss Switch!"

"Sssss!" Bathsheba hissed at me. "Can't you see she's busy thinking?" It didn't look as if Bathsheba's disposition had grown any better since I last saw her.

Miss Switch finally looked up. "Mind your manners, cat!" She shot a fierce spark right onto Bathsheba's nose.

"Br-o-o-owl!" howled Bathsheba, brushing her nose with her paw.

"There's more where that came from!" Miss Switch snapped. "Good evening, Rupert!" Miss Switch nodded at me, but went right back to studying the eraser. Finding nothing better to do with myself, I peeled off my jacket and pulled off my earmuffs.

"Blast and botheration!" Miss Switch muttered. "I thought I'd have this thing figured out by now. If I don't do it soon, it might take us forever to find Amelia. Forever is a long time, Rupert, even for a second-rate warlock like Mordo."

"What are you trying to figure out, Miss Switch?" I asked anxiously. *Forever* sounded like a pretty long time to me, too.

"Why, this confounded eraser isn't working the way it should, Rupert. I performed a perfectly good bewitching on it a few minutes ago, but it's behavior barely rates a D-minus."

I hesitated. "Miss Switch—er—I guess I

74

really don't know what it is you're talking about. What's bewitching a blackboard eraser got to do with finding Amelia?''

Miss Switch drummed her long fingers on the desk impatiently. ''It so happens, Rupert, that you cannot bewitch a blackboard without first bewitching a blackboard eraser. Or if you want to put it in one of your more modern terms, the blackboard has to be activated by the eraser. Is that clear?''

''It sounds reasonable,'' I replied. ''On the other hand, Miss Switch, what's the blackboard got to do with anything?''

Miss Switch sighed with despair over my ignorance. ''Rupert, it is the *blackboard,* ordinarily a means of delivering information to the fifth grade, which, properly bewitched or activated, might also deliver information about Amelia, wherever she may be. But as I will now demonstrate, something is out of whack, or sync, if you'd rather.''

With that, Miss Switch began to swoop back and forth, swishing the eraser across the blackboard. Swoop, swish! Swoop, swish! Swoop, swish! To my amazement, the blackboard began to glow strangely, like a television tube just before the picture comes on. Then shadows began moving about, as if a picture were trying to come through, but not quite making it. Still, it was a mind-bending experience to see my ordinary old blackboard, that had never done

anything magical about the fifth grade's arithmetic mistakes or misspelled words, suddenly
performing like this.

"Wow!" I said.

"Wow, nothing!" snorted Miss Switch. "It
might be *wow* if we could actually see anything,
but this is as good as it's going to get, unfortunately."

"Maybe you should try another eraser," I
suggested hopefully.

"For your information, Rupert, this *is* another eraser. The fourth one, actually. Must be
some of those confounded new synthetic fibers
present. They can wreak havoc with some of
the old tried-and-true spells." Miss Switch
paused a moment, and then began waving her
arms over the Bunsen burner, intoning these
words:

"Though far or near,
Bright and clear,
Bring back the thing that's disappeared.
Fog begone, shine moonlight bright,
Let pictures through the black of night.
Ricketty, racketty, hullaballoo,
Amelia Daley, please come through!"

The last part of this spell sounded more like
something you'd hear from the Pepperdine
cheering team, but as spells go, it probably
wasn't all that bad. "That sounds okay to me,
Miss Switch."

"Likewise," said Miss Switch.

"You know," I said, "the last time you did a bewitching, you had some stuff like wing of bat and eye of newt. I know you don't believe a lot in those things, but I happened to bring a couple of old toadstools along with me, just in case."

"You're right, Rupert, I don't put much stock in those old-fashioned remedies. But let me have a look at them, anyway."

I fished the toadstools from my pocket and handed them to her. She studied them both for a few moments, then handed one back to me.

"I don't think this one is of any use to us now, but it has some very strange and interesting, though puzzling, qualities. I suggest you keep it."

For some reason that I can't explain, I shoved the toadstool into my desk instead of my pants' pocket, and promptly forgot all about it. Miss Switch continued to study the other toadstool. I could see that this one really interested her. She had her face practically on it as she examined it.

"Where did you get this, Rupert?"

"I found them both in the Pepperdine playground. They were left over from the football bewitching."

Miss Switch looked up at me, her eyes crackling with excitement. "Out of quintillion toadstools in this world, give or take a couple, only one might possibly be of this variety. And you,

Rupert, have found one, a *Toadstoolius black-boardius bewitchicum!*"

"You're kidding!" I said.

"Not at all, Rupert. And I might add it was very clever of you to think of bringing the toad-stools."

"I have to be honest, Miss Switch. It was Guinevere, my guinea pig, who thought of it, not me."

"Well, my compliments to Guinevere! I'm glad you have a clever animal like that watching over you, Rupert. But now, let's get on with this."

I watched, fascinated, as Miss Switch crumbled the rare *Toadstoolius blackboardius bewitchicum* into a fine powder, and sprinkled it on the eraser. A moment later, the eraser began to give off an eerie glow.

"Aha!" Miss Switch gave a triumphant shout. She picked up the eraser and began to swoop and swoosh over the blackboard as she had before.

But this time, the shadows on the blackboard began to take shape, becoming clearer and clearer until, at last, we were looking at an old sailing vessel that looked like a large version of the one in the bottle. Something else, too. We could hear water lapping against the ship. Sound as well as sight!

"Wow, Miss Switch!" I shouted. "This is just like live television!"

"Exactly!" said Miss Switch.

Hypnotized, I watched as the blackboard picture moved toward the stern of the ship. Now we could read its name, and learned that this was the good ship *Bide-A-Wee*.

"*Bide-A-Wee!*" I exclaimed. "What kind of name is that for a ship, Miss Switch?"

"A very friendly term meaning generally 'come on in and stay a while.' And if this is indeed Mordo's ship," Miss Switch added sternly, "then I suspect that, in his guise as Captain Mordecai, he invited unsuspecting townspeople aboard for his toad bewitchments."

"Murderation!" I breathed in horror.

"Precisely!" said Miss Switch.

Next, the picture took us over the ship's rail onto the wooden deck, and it appeared to be absolutely deserted. There wasn't even anyone around on night watch. And something else was curious, too. This was the filthiest, most dilapidated-looking ship I had ever seen in my whole life, and a far cry from that spit-and polish little ship in the bottle. The sails were tattered and torn, the brass was tarnished, the iron chains were rusted, and the deck was strewn with frayed ropes, ragged pieces of cloth, and even potato peels and eggshells. In other words, garbage!

"Ugh!" I said.

"You couldn't have found a better word, Rupert," said Miss Switch.

The picture didn't dwell on this disaster area for very long, however, but moved right along through a doorway and down some steep steps. Then it went through another doorway and down more steps into a room that must have been at the very bottom of the ship.

In the room was a long table on which sat dozens of bottles and jars of all shapes and sizes, and one huge, thick book. A tall man in a black cape was leaning so far over the book that his face was quite hidden, furiously thumbing through the pages. Standing to one side, with a hawk perched on his shoulders, was a squatty, humpbacked little man not much taller than the table itself. With a big bulb of a nose, squinty eyes, and hair that stood up like porcupine quills, this individual looked more like a troll than a human person. As the picture focused on these two for a moment, the tall man looked up suddenly, and we had a clear view of his scowling face.

"Mordo!" I gasped.

"One and the same!" said Miss Switch. "And second-rate he may be, Rupert, but I agree with you that he certainly looks scary enough."

We hardly had time to study Mordo's wicked face, however, before the picture suddenly changed to a shot of one of the walls, and began

80

slowly revolving around the room. Then I gasped again. What had at first looked like just a bunch of shelves were actually cages. And inside the cages were toads! I couldn't even guess how many, but they were packed in there wall-to-wall, croaking their heads off and struggling to get out.

Was one of them Amelia? I strained my eyes desperately to see if any toad had something about it that looked familiar. Then, all at once, the picture focused on the floor in one corner of the room. And there—no, not in the shape of a toad, but in the same familiar shape I had known for the better part of my life, with the same curls and the same three freckles on her nose—was the formerly vanished, but clearly very much alive (even though clearly very much scared), Amelia Matilda Daley!

9

Mordo Makes a Boo-Boo

"Omigosh! Omigosh!" I began jumping up and down like a jack-in-the-box, waving my arms about. "There's Amelia! That's Amelia, Miss Switch!"

"Quite so, Rupert!" Miss Switch sounded calm enough, but I knew she was just as happy as I was.

"Well, now that we know where she is, can we go get her?" I made a dive for my jacket and earmuffs, ready to take off.

"Rupert, all we know is that Amelia is on the good ship *Bide-A-Wee*. But where it is, and even *when* it is, have not yet been established. What I'm hoping is that, by our watching carefully and listening, this information will be revealed. Now, pay attention! Mordo looks as if he is about to speak."

Mordo sure was. "Blast! Blast! Double Blast!" He pounded on the table.

"You be not able to find anything, eh, master?" said the troll-like person.

"Not a blasted thing! Blast! No salves, no ointments, no pills or potions. Just plain, blasted nothing, Mildew. You'd think after all these years someone would have come up with a little remedy to restore toad powers once they've gone rusty."

"Yes, you would be thinking that, master." Mildew nodded his porcupine head.

"Aw-aw-awk!" said the hawk.

"Oh, do shut your beak, Smauk!" snarled Mordo. "All these years I've owned you and still all you can say is 'aw-aw-awk.' I should stew you for my dinner and get myself another pet."

Mildew quickly put Smauk protectively under his arm. "He be only trying to tell you he be agreeing with you, master."

"And well he might!" said Mordo dismally. "He knows what *she* might do to me if I don't keep my end of the bargain and turn that scientific little busybody over there on the floor into a toad. Not to mention her scientific little busybody boyfriend. Aaaargh! I'd like to get my hands on him right now."

"W-w-we're not scientific little busybodies!" blurted Amelia's brave, but scared, voice from the corner of the room. "W-w-we're great scientists. You'd better be careful what you say!"

"And you'd better mind your manners, if you know what's good for you!" roared Mordo.

"Boy!" I said to Miss Switch. "*He* should talk. If you want to know, I sure don't think Mordo's manners are all that hot."

"Abominable!" said Miss Switch.

We concentrated again on the blackboard.

"Be the boy having powerful magic protecting him, master?" asked Mildew.

"That he does, Mildew," replied Mordo. "It's called a *Saxophonius gruesomus*. Makes the worst noises you ever heard in your life. I could rule the world with that sound, and some day I mean to get my hands on it."

"N-n-no you won't!" cried Amelia. "Rupert will never let you!"

"Aaaargh!" Mordo snarled at her. "When the two of you are toads, there'll be nothing to stop me."

"What be you thinking *she* be doing to you, master, if you be not turning them into toads?" Mildew asked anxiously.

Mordo turned his back to Amelia and lowered his voice. "Somehow she'll find a way to get me back into that blasted bottle! She can probably do it, too. She's a powerful witch."

"So what be you going to do now, master?"

"Practice!" Mordo groaned. "I must transform someone from this century to find if my toad-turning touch has gone rusty like everything else on this blasted ship."

"Who be you going to practice on, master?" Mildew jerked a finger at the toad cages. "All your crew be used up, and nobody be wanting to sign up because all be afraid of disappearing. Also, master, this ship now be named the good ship *Pig Sty*, and nobody be wanting even to come visit anymore."

"I know," said Mordo gloomily. "I shall have to go ashore and do the best I can. You remain here, Mildew, and tend the toads. I shall return as quickly as possible with a subject." With that, Mordo stomped up the stairs, changing as he did into the crusty (but twinkly-eyed), Captain Mordecai.

"The better to capture some unsuspecting victim!" I breathed to Miss Switch in horror.

"Yes, yes, of course, Rupert," said Miss Switch impatiently. Her mind seemed to be off somewhere in space. *"She,* eh? Who do they mean by *she?"*

"Golly, Miss Switch," I said, "Mordo was talking about some *she* when he came out of the bottle. He wouldn't tell us who it was, but I just figured he meant the witch who delivered the bottle."

"It might be Gulldemonia, Rupert, although why she would want to harm you and Amelia is a mystery to me. And why employ Mordo to do the dirty work? Hmmm!" Miss Switch's eyes narrowed.

Further thoughts anyone might have on the

mysterious *she* were cut short, however, by the sudden appearance through the door of a young boy about Amelia's and my age, skipping happily down the steps ahead of Captain Mordecai.

Mildew grinned. "You had good luck, master. He be a good specimen for the toad bewitching practice."

"Toad bewitching!" The boy's eyes popped. He whirled around, but found that his way out was blocked, not by Captain Mordecai, but by Mordo! "Thou—thou art a warlock!"

"Very intelligent lad," sneered Mordo.

"And thou hast lied!" the boy cried. "Thou art not bringing me here to show me thy toad collection. Thou art going to turn me into one!"

"However did you guess?" said Mordo. Then he snatched the kicking, struggling boy up under his arm. "Here, Mildew, tie him up like the other one while I prepare for the bewitching."

In a matter of moments, the boy was bound hand and foot, and tossed off into the corner with Amelia like a sack of potatoes.

Back in the Pepperdine Elementary School's fifth-grade classroom, I began to shout. "Miss Switch! Miss Switch! We've got to get there, wherever *there* is, and rescue them before it's too late."

"Don't you think I know that, Rupert?" said Miss Switch sternly. "But wherever *there* is, is exactly the problem. We can't just go flitting about on my broomstick through eternity and infinity, blindly looking for the right century and the right place. You had better transmit those powerful thoughtwaves of yours to Amelia in the hope that she will reveal what we need to know.''

"Right, Miss Switch!" I took a deep breath and concentrated as hard as I ever had in my life in waving out powerful thoughts.

"Amelia," said my thoughts, "please ask him where you are, and when you are. Otherwise it may be Toadsville for the two of you. Please, Amelia!" I held my breath and waited.

"How didst thou get here?" the boy whispered to Amelia.

"It's a very long story," Amelia whispered back. "I don't think there's time to tell you now. You wouldn't believe it, anyway."

"Well, what is thy name, then?"

"Amelia Daley. What's yours?"

"Thaddeus Partlow, and if thou wilt excuse me for saying so, thou talkest in a passing strange manner. Thou dressest very oddly, also."

"The way you talk and dress is funny to me, too, Thaddeus," said Amelia. "Could—could you tell me, please, what year this is, and where we are?"

I looked triumphantly at Miss Switch. Boy, did I have powerful thoughtwaves!

"Thou must certainly attend a curious

school," Thaddeus said to Amelia. "One that does not even teach thee where thou art living, and when. What school dost thou attend?"

"Pepperdine Elementary, but this isn't their fault. They didn't know I was going to be here, wherever *here* is, and when."

"Pepperdine? What a curious name," said Thaddeus. "Well, if thou really dost not know where thou art, or the year, I shall tell thee. Thou art—"

Back at Pepperdine, I lunged for pencil and paper from Miss Switch's desk. But I might as well have saved my energy on that exercise (not to mention those powerful thoughtwaves).

"Silence!" roared Mordo. And before I even had a chance to groan, "Oh, heck!" he had started on his bewitching act before an admiring Mildew, and a scared Thaddeus and Amelia.

By then I guess I'd seen enough bewitchings to know what to expect, but this time Mordo really did put on a show. Swoop! Swoosh! Mumbo jumbo! His black cloak flew out as he swept around the room. The performance went on and on. And in the end, when Mordo leaned against his table, worn out and gasping for air, he had indeed succeeded in adding another toad to the room. Except it wasn't Thaddeus. And it wasn't Amelia, either.

The new toad was sitting on Mildew's shoulder. "Aw-aw-awk!" it croaked.

You guessed it—Mordo had made a boo-boo,

and somehow managed to turn his pet bird into a toad!

"Smauk! Smauk! What have I done? I didn't mean that about stewing you for my dinner!" Mordo was practically sobbing. "Oh, woe!" It was easy to see that Mordo was really pretty crazy about that bird. I almost felt sorry for him.

"Be you not worried, master," Mildew said cheerfully. "You just be doing another bewitching and soon Smauk be back a bird, like before."

"Oh no, Mildew, I can't do it," moaned Mordo.

"Oh *yes,* master! You be able to do it later when you be rested."

Mordo wrung his hands. "Rest has nothing to do with it. When I say I can't do it, I mean I don't know how! Once a toad, always a toad. Oh, poor Smauk!"

And it was then that Amelia giggled. I had to admire her bravery. In her position, I would have been scared spitless. On the other hand, giggling at that point wasn't too smart. Mordo suddenly stopped worrying about his bird to concentrate on growing purple with rage.

"Aaargh! Aaargh! Aaargh!" Mordo gnashed his teeth furiously. "Just wait until your turn comes, and come it will. You won't think it so funny when I've changed *you* into toads, and you know you can never be changed back again. Aaargh!'' He began to sweep around the room again. "This time I'll be successful. You mark my words!"

"Omigosh, Miss Switch!" I cried. "This is awful!"

"It is very serious indeed, Rupert." Miss Switch stared gravely into the flickering flame of the Bunsen burner. "I've had it in the back of my head all along that if Amelia or Thaddeus had already been turned into a toad, I could use my not-insignificant powers to persuade Mordo to reverse the bewitchment, and now I discover that he doesn't know how."

"Oh, murder!" I groaned.

"In a nutshell!" said Miss Switch.

"Couldn't you de-toad Amelia and Thaddeus yourself, Miss Switch?" I asked.

She shook her head. "Reversing someone else's bewitchment is very tricky, even if you have learned the proper incantations and formulas from the original bewitcher. If the bewitcher himself, like this second-rate warlock, doesn't know them—well, you can see the problem, Rupert."

"Boy, can I ever! Miss Switch, what are we going to do now? Things are getting worse and worse."

"We have no choice but to take off on my broomstick, and pray," replied Miss Switch grimly. "If only I knew where to begin the search."

90

"How about the fifth-grade history book?" said Bathsheba. She had been sitting on the teacher's desk this whole time, calmly giving herself a bath.

"Don't play games with me now, cat!" snapped Miss Switch. "This is no time for humor."

"I'm not playing games." Bathsheba scrubbed her whiskers daintily with one paw. "I just think you should start your search by looking in Rupert's history book."

"I don't know what she's talking about, Rupert," said Miss Switch impatiently. "But I have some serious thinking to do about our itinerary, so we'll humor her, anyway. Get out your history book, please!"

It seemed to me that it was more useful to keep an eye on Mordo than to dig through an old, beat-up, fifth-grade history book. But an order from Miss Switch was an order from Miss Switch, and I wasn't going to argue. I pulled the book from my desk, flicked off a dried lump of peanut butter (dropped there by me from a former peanut-butter sandwich), and opened the cover.

"Where should I begin?" I asked.

"At the beginning, of course," said Bathsheba sourly. "Where do you begin anything?"

So while Mordo swooped across the blackboard, and Miss Switch paced in front of the teacher's desk, I thumbed through the pages of my history book. I had about decided that this was really a terrible waste of time, when, all at once, the flickering light of the Bunsen burner fell on the picture of a very interesting painting. The painting was of a small town beside the sea, with a ship anchored alongside it. My heart began to jump peculiarly. I made a dive for the small magnifying glass on the teacher's desk, and focused it on the ship.

"Omigosh! Omigosh!" I gasped under my breath. "It's Mordo's ship!"

Now, I have to admit that the tatters-and-rags appearance of the ship we had seen on the blackboard made it hard to find any connection with the shining, spit-and-polish little ship in the picture. But I had proof positive that they were one and the same ship, because there on the stern, in letters so tiny they looked like pinpricks to the naked eye, were the words *Bide-A-Wee!* To think that I'd been looking at old Mordo's ship right in my history book all this time and hadn't even known it.

I started to leap around, waving the book under Miss Switch's nose. "Look, Miss Switch! Look!"

"Astonishing!" she exclaimed as she peered through the magnifying glass.

Then we both read the words under the picture. "Typical sailing vessel of the period *circa* 1640, shown docked at a port on the rocky coast of Maine."

"Does that give us enough information, Miss Switch?" I asked anxiously.

"Quite enough, Rupert!" replied Miss Switch. Then she looked sternly at Bathsheba. "Why didn't you tell us this before, cat?"

"You never asked me," replied Bathsheba with an injured air.

"Hmmmph!" snorted Miss Switch, but she gave Bathsheba a scratch behind the ear, anyway.

"Are we going to leave now?" I grabbed up my jacket and earmuffs.

"At once!" Miss Switch picked up the eraser, and with an angry swipe, wiped Mordo right off the blackboard. Personally, I was glad to see him disappear.

Miss Switch took her broomstick, which was leaning against the fifth-grade best-work board, and started for the window. But before she reached it, she hesitated. "Rupert, this could be dangerous. You don't have to go if you don't wish to, you know."

I drew back my shoulders and raised my chin. "I'm going, Miss Switch! Besides," I went on cheerily, "I wouldn't miss another broomstick ride for anything."

Miss Switch's left eyebrow flew up. "Be forewarned, Rupert, that this ride will be nothing like the other one. Going back in time is something entirely different from merely romping around in space."

93

"I'm going, Miss Switch!" I repeated firmly.

"Very well, then," said Miss Switch. "I'm happy to see that you had the foresight to bring your earmuffs. You'll need them."

I decided that I would keep to myself the information that the earmuffs, as well as the toadstools, were Guinevere's idea. I was beginning to feel a little embarrassed about a guinea pig being smarter than I was.

"Come to think of it," Miss Switch said, "Amelia, if already bewitched, can ride in your pocket. If not, she will also need something warm to protect her against the rigors of time and space travel. See what you can find in the class lost-and-found cupboard, Rupert."

I didn't waste a moment worrying about the horrors of Amelia being reduced to the size of something that would fit in my pocket, but quickly looked for and found a set of regular, Amelia-size earmuffs and jacket. In the meantime, with a flick of her tail, Bathsheba leaped from the teacher's desk onto the windowsill. Then she, Miss Switch, and I boarded the broomstick.

As we took off from the window ledge, Miss Switch threw her head back with the same wild, cackling laugh she had used on our last broomstick ride. My ears may have been warm, but my insides grew chilly at this reminder that, after all, Miss Switch was still a witch. And I was going with her to a place where there was no more Pepperdine Elementary School; no more Mr. and Mrs. Rupert P. Brown Jr. (my mother and father); no more Peatmouse, Banana, and Creampuff; no more Caruso, Hector, and Guinevere; and not even any more Detective Plume, who might end up looking for Amelia *and* me forever.

I have to admit that, brave though I might have appeared, my heart was lodged somewhere in the neighborhood of my throat as our broomstick zoomed across the playground, and into the night.

10

On the Good Ship
Bide-A-Wee

Miss Switch was certainly right about this broomstick ride being different from the other! If I'd known what it was really going to be like, I might not have been quite so cheery about it.

In my earlier account, I wrote about stars twinkling above us, and the lights of tall buildings twinkling below. There was a big, round moon which looked like either (Amelia and I couldn't decide) an orange or a pale persimmon. We saw laundry flying off into the sky like white birds when Miss Switch undid the clothespins, and apples flying into the air like miniature gold and red balloons when Miss Switch shook the trees. It was only at the end that our ride became spooky, with mist swirling around Witch's Mountain, blacking out the stars and turning the moon into a cold, green eye of ice.

But on this trip there was no moon at all, and no stars, and no lights from tall buildings down below. It was just pitch, pitch darkness from the moment we took off.

I could sure *feel* things, though. Like my ears popping when the broomstick took a sudden, scary dip, or going from blistering hot to cold that felt like it had to be a zillion degrees below.

Sometimes, when it was so hot it seemed as if we had to be right up against something as hot as the sun, my skin felt as if it were stretching. It seemed to grow thinner and thinner, just like a balloon that's having air blown into it. And about the time I thought I was going to explode, "pop" would go my ears inside my earmuffs, and I'd shrink back down to Rupert P. Brown III-size again.

Most of the time, though, we were flying through miserable, freezing cold. Then my skin felt as if it were a huge, wet, icy glove that was shrinking and shrinking, getting smaller and smaller with me inside it. A zillion degrees below? Make that ten zillion!

"You can understand why I'm glad you brought your earmuffs!" Miss Switch hollered back at me.

"Y-y-you b-b-bet, M-M-Miss S-S-Switch!" I yelled through chattering teeth. I felt as if my words were being blown right out of my mouth into the tailwash of the broomstick, and that she didn't even hear them. Otherwise I might

have mentioned that she ought to have suggested that I bring muffs for a few other parts
of my body!

Then suddenly I seemed to stop shrinking
and stretching. It was still pretty cold, but more
like an ordinary winter day, and my skin felt
like my old, familiar skin again. I was pretty
certain that something different had now taken
place in our flight, so I wasn't too surprised
when Miss Switch shouted, "I think we're almost there, Rupert. At least we're finished with
our journey through time. Now all we have to
worry about is space, so keep a sharp lookout
below."

I peered down through the clouds and couldn't
see a thing but darkness. It was late at night,
but shouldn't there still be lights twinkling
down below? And then I remembered—this
was 1640! There would be no tall buildings, no
street lights, no *electricity*. How would we ever
find Mordo's ship in all that darkness? Clouds
brushed past us as our broomstick cruised
slowly up the coastline, but all we saw was
rocks and trees, and the whitecaps of waves
dashing against the shore. It was spooky and
desolate.

And then all at once Bathsheba gave a howl.
"Br-r-o-owl!" Her sharp eyes had seen the
lonely little light way below us, swaying in the
offshore breeze.

"Hold on, everyone!" Miss Switch shouted, and we zoomed down.

The light was from a ship, all right. Miss Switch took the broomstick around the stern and there it was—*Bide-A-Wee!* I felt my heart flip over. Here was the very ship we'd seen on the blackboard, and Amelia was inside it.

I thought we were going to go aboard at once, but instead, Miss Switch took the broomstick on a slow turn around the ship. It looked as bad as it had on the blackboard, all ragged and tattered and rusted and strewn with garbage. What a mess! I could only suppose that the picture in the fifth-grade history book had been done in the ship's early days before Mordo had turned all his crew into toads. But then I wasn't particularly interested in a guided tour of the good ship *Pig Sty*. I wanted to get on with the business of rescuing Amelia.

"In case you're wondering why we're not rushing right in, Rupert," said Miss Switch, reading my mind, "it's because I don't want to walk in without planning our strategy. Mordo may be second-rate, but he's still a warlock. I must say I'd feel much safer if we didn't have to go down into that hold, and could make a quick escape on the broomstick. The question is, what step to take first."

Miss Switch had no sooner posed the question, than she had her answer. The door leading onto the deck burst open, and out stepped

Mordo and Mildew. Miss Switch almost left me behind in the air as she took the broomstick on a sudden nosedive right under the gangplank. The toes of my sneakers trailed in the water as we hovered there silently in mid-air. It was so deadly quiet that we could hear Mordo and Mildew's voices clearly.

"It be very late, master," Mildew said. "How be you going to find another one at this hour?"

"We'll just comb the streets of the settlement," said Mordo grimly. "Some simpleton will be wandering around, no doubt."

"If you be saying so, master," replied Mildew.

Their voices faded as they thumped on down the gangplank right over our heads, and off down the shore.

"Well!" snorted Miss Switch. "Speaking of simpletons, those two have certainly made our job a lot easier. Now we have no one to tangle with. And if they are off looking for another subject, their bewitchment of Thaddeus must have failed. So all we have to do, Rupert, is pick up Amelia, free Thaddeus, and be on our way!"

I nearly flew off the broomstick a second time as we whizzed out from under the gangplank and onto the deck. The broomstick parked by the ship's rail, Miss Switch, Bathsheba, and I threaded our way through the glop and the goo

100

on the deck, and then crept down the stairs.
But the door to the lower room was padlocked.
How were we going to get through that? I wondered, forgetting that if Mordo was a warlock,
Miss Switch was a witch. The lock fell apart
like melting butter in her hands, and the next
thing I knew, we were descending the stairs
into the room where Amelia was held prisoner.
And there she was, still lying in the corner,
bound hand and foot, and staring at us with the
widest eyes you ever saw in your life.

"Miss Switch! Rupert! Bathsheba! Oh! Oh!
Oh!"

I was at her side in a flash, untying the knots.
Now, this part of my story gets a little embar-
rassing, but in the interest of scientific accuracy, I have to report everything. The fact is
that Amelia and I then hugged each other. And,
having mentioned this, I will now move quickly
on with my story.

"Oh, Miss Switch and Rupert, I'm so glad
you found me!" Amelia cried. Then she jumped
up and threw her arms around Miss Switch.
You may remember from my earlier account
that Amelia had done this once before, and I
had nearly fainted. I nearly did again. It's not
easy to get used to the idea of anyone hugging
a witch.

It's my opinion that witches are not used to
the idea of anyone hugging witches either.
Also, that it is important for them not to look

101

as though they like it. "Tut, tut, Amelia! Enough of this!" Miss Switch made a big attempt to look disapproving. "We have more important things to attend to."

"Like rescuing you and Thaddeus!" I burst in.

Amelia gasped. "How did you know about Thaddeus?"

"That's a long story, Amelia," I said. "I'll tell you all about it later. But where is he?"

Before Amelia could reply, a terrible racket broke out on top of Mordo's table.

"Aw-aw-awk!"

"Sssssssss!"

Bathsheba was on the table, her back arched and the fur of her black tail standing out like a bottle brush, hissing at one of two toads crouching amidst all the bottles and jars.

"Aw-aw-aw-awk!" croaked the toad, formerly Smauk.

"Sssssssssssss!" hissed Bathsheba.

"Gribbet! Gribbet!" croaked the second toad. "Wouldst thou help me, please? I'm Thaddeus." He sounded, if you'll pardon me for saying so, as if he had a frog in his throat. But you could understand him if you listened carefully.

Miss Switch quickly separated Bathsheba and Smauk, while I scooped Thaddeus up in my hands. "Omigosh, Miss Switch!" I moaned. "We're too late! Thaddeus," I said to him, "we were going to help you escape when we rescued Amelia, but we hoped you'd still be a boy and not a toad."

"Thou art very kind," croaked Thaddeus. "B-b-but is that not a witch thou art with? Will she not turn thee into a toad, too?"

"Certainly not!" snapped Miss Switch. "The very idea!"

"Miss Switch is a friendly witch who sometimes is our fifth-grade substitute teacher at Pepperdine," I explained to Thaddeus. "At any rate, at least Mordo didn't bewitch Amelia. I wonder why?"

"He tried!" Amelia said angrily. "He just couldn't do it, that's all."

"It appears, Amelia," Miss Switch said, "that you and Rupert are being protected from toad bewitchment by some mysterious force. For the moment, I believe you are both safe."

"But what about Thaddeus?" I cried. "Is he going to have to stay a toad forever?"

"Not if we can find a way for Mordo to reverse his toad bewitchments, Rupert. If we do, we can help not only Thaddeus, but all these poor creatures as well." Miss Switch pointed to the cages. The toads all looked back at us helplessly, occasionally giving off a croak that I could now tell were really the words, "Help! Help!" It was pretty pitiful.

"You know," Miss Switch continued, "there is no such thing as a bewitchment where the bewitchee cannot be bewitched back, one way or another.''

"But what's the use of Mordo knowing the way to reverse the bewitchments if he won't use it?" I asked.

"He must be persuaded," said Miss Switch, looking grim.

She drummed her long fingers on Mordo's table, casting sharp glances around the room. Then she went into deep thought, staring absently at the huge book lying open, just as Mordo had left it. Amelia, Thaddeus, and I watched her in intent silence, knowing that Thaddeus' future lay in her hands. Suddenly, something in the book caught her attention. She began to read furiously, her lips moving as if she were talking to herself. On and on she read, whipping through the pages of the book.

The minutes ticked by. I was beginning to get a little nervous about the possibility of Mordo and Mildew returning, but Miss Switch was in charge, and I didn't want to bother her. More minutes ticked by, so Amelia, Thaddeus, and I began to whisper amongst ourselves. We had a lot to whisper about!

First, I wanted to know from Amelia what it felt like to vanish, only to learn they hadn't vanished at all! It had just been a Mordo-was-quicker-than-the-eye routine. He had merely opened the window and jumped out with Amelia, which naturally explained the draft of cold air I felt. Then he had pulled a branch from our oak tree to use as a makeshift broomstick. It provided a very bumpy ride, Amelia said, during which she wasn't sure whether she was going to die from fright, or cold.

"Wow, Amelia!" I said. "And to think I was complaining about not having more extra padding than just my earmuffs."

"But how didst thou find Amelia?" croaked Thaddeus. "And how didst thou know about me?"

"We knew about you through the fifth-grade blackboard, which Miss Switch bewitched into showing us a moving, talking picture, just like television," I explained. "Then we found out exactly where Mordo's ship was through a picture in our fifth-grade history book."

"Was it anything like that one?" Amelia pointed to a painting hanging directly over our heads, that I had missed entirely in all the excitement.

"Amelia, it's a photograph of that exact painting!" I exclaimed under my breath.

We looked at one another in amazement.

Thaddeus gave a polite, hesitant croak. "Wouldst either of thee like to explain what a photograph is or—or this television of which thou speakest? Are these perhaps specialties of this strange school known as Pepperdine, which failest to teach its pupils where they are, or when?"

Omigosh! I had all but forgotten that, though we knew quite a lot about the seventeenth century from our history class, Thaddeus couldn't know anything about a century that hadn't taken place yet when he was in school. In fact, he didn't even know we were from another century, so that was the first thing we had to tell him.

But can anyone imagine how complicated it is to describe the twentieth century to someone from the seventeenth century? Even when we told Thaddeus how we came to meet Miss Switch because she got sent to Pepperdine by the Comput-o-witch, I had to explain that this was a computer for witches.

"But couldst thou please explain what is a computer?" croaked Thaddeus.

You can see the problem. Amelia and I did the best we could, however, whispering so fast our words were tumbling all over each other. Strangely enough, though, what seemed to interest Thaddeus the most was that one of my best friends had the same name he did—Partlow—and was probably one of his descendants.

"And thou sayest that thou hast named him Peatmouse?" Thaddeus chuckled (or I should say, croaked). "That name doth please me immensely. If I ever return to my school, I wish that my friend, Jeremiah, wouldst call me that, too."

While all this was going on, the time was

slipping away, of course, and I began to get nervous again. I handed Thaddeus to Amelia, and started toward Miss Switch. But I had only taken two steps when she looked up from the book with a funny look in her eyes.

"Rupert, let me see that other toadstool you found at Pepperdine, please."

"I don't have it, Miss Switch. I stuck it in my desk back at school."

Miss Switch scowled. "Botheration! I'll have to go and fetch it."

"And—and leave us here?" I asked.

"Don't be ridiculous, Rupert! We came here to rescue Amelia, not to dispose of the two of you. But if the toadstool is what I think it is, and if these toads are to be returned to their natural selves, then I must return with it. That toadstool, if what I have learned from this book is correct, may be the one special ingredient that would allow Mordo to reverse his toad bewitchments."

"I didn't know there was a special ingredient," I said.

"Nor did I. But it seems that there is. It is a toadstool far rarer even than the *Toadstoolius blackboardius bewitchicum*. There are probably no more than one in septillion. But you, Rupert, unless I miss my guess, have found it, a *Toadstoolius toadus reversicum!*"

"Yikes!" I said.

"And well you may say that!" returned Miss

Switch. "But now we must not dally another moment. Come along, Rupert and Amelia! Hurry up, Bathsheba!" She marched to the stairs.

"But what about Thaddeus?" Amelia asked. "We can't just leave him here."

"*Here,* Amelia, is where I shall return to persuade Mordo to reverse his bewitchments. Helping the toads to escape now, or taking Thaddeus with us, will do no good at all."

"Oh, prithee please, Mistress Switch," croaked Thaddeus, "take me with thee. Should Rupert's toadstool not be a *Toadstoolius toadus reversicum* as thou thinkest, thou wouldst have no reason to return. I cannot go home, because my mother and father wouldst not believe their son had become a talking toad. Being fearful of witchcraft in general, they wouldst most likely dump me into a vat of boiling water. Thus my ending wouldst be most painful as well as final."

"He's right, Miss Switch!" I cried. "Please, could we take him?"

"All right then," said Miss Switch. "Bring him along!"

As soon as Amelia and I had zipped ourselves into our jackets and put on our earmuffs, I picked Thaddeus up and thrust him into my jacket pocket. Then the four of us (five if you counted Thaddeus in my pocket) hurried up the stairs. Boy, I thought, was I ever glad to be getting out of that place! Especially without bumping into Mordo.

We had no sooner stepped through the doorway onto the deck, however, than we heard footsteps stumping up the gangplank. The footsteps were accompanied by two familiar figures, arriving back on the deck of the good ship *Bide-A-Wee* after what seemed to be a fruitless search for a new toad-bewitching subject.

"M-M-Mordo!" I gasped.

"W-w-with M-M-Mildew!" moaned Amelia.

Naturally, the first thing the two of them saw was the four of us (not counting Thaddeus in my pocket), getting ready to board the broomstick.

Mordo's face twisted with rage as he recognized Amelia and me. "What's going on here?" Then he saw that we were with Miss Switch. "You!" he snarled. "What are you doing here, Sabbatina Switch?"

"That is *Miss* Switch to you, Mordo," replied Miss Switch frostily. "And what I am doing is retrieving a part of my fifth-grade class. Now, if you don't mind, we have things to attend to. Come along, students, climb on the broomstick."

Amelia and I lost no time in climbing. I could tell that Miss Switch was nervous, not about herself, of course, but about us, although she gave no sign of it to Mordo. She appeared cool as a cat's eyes.

"Y-y-you give them back to me! G-g-give them back at once!" sputtered Mordo, almost speechless with rage. But when he saw that Miss Switch had no intention of bringing back anything, he tried another tack. "Come, come," he said smoothly, "why don't you come back in and we can talk all this over like two sensible witches."

"I might just do that—after I have returned Amelia and Rupert," replied Miss Switch briskly.

"But it's them I want, not you," whined Mordo, forgetting himself. "I can't do anything to you."

"Exactly!" snapped Miss Switch, throwing a leg over the broomstick.

His temper lost once and for all, Mordo shook his fist at us. *"She'll* see that you pay for this!"

Miss Switch sniffed disdainfully. "And who, may I ask, is *she?"*

"That's none of your business!" growled Mordo. "But *she'll* get you, all of you!"

"More than likely it's *you* she'll get, Mordo, whoever *she* is," replied Miss Switch calmly.

Mordo clutched his chest, and his green skin grew even greener. It was easy to see that he agreed entirely with Miss Switch's conclusion. But he recovered himself at once. "You won't get away with this!" he screamed. "The next

110

time it won't be just the two of them. I'll get your whole precious Pepperdine fifth grade!''

"Pfaw!" said Miss Switch. "Now, hang on, children, the sooner we leave this *garbage scow* the better!" Then she gave the broomstick a shove with her foot, and we sailed off the deck of the *Bide-A-Wee*.

"Garbage scow? *Garbage* scow!" Mordo was choking with rage. We could still hear him ranting and screaming as we took off into the darkness on our way back to the twentieth century and Pepperdine. But my stomach was still tied into a big, tight knot, because I had the terrible feeling that I had not seen the last of Captain Mordecai, alias Mordo the warlock, or the good ship *Bide-A-Wee*.

11

The Whole Pepperdine Elementary School Fifth Grade

"Now, Rupert, the toadstool, please!" commanded Miss Switch the moment we had climbed through the window of the fifth-grade classroom at Pepperdine.

After quickly removing Thaddeus from my pocket and setting him down on the teacher's desk, I ran to my desk. After several nervous moments spent digging through a couple of old erasers, three chewed-up pencils, some ancient arithmetic papers, and a dried-up apple core Peatmouse had deposited there one day (because he was too lazy to take it to the trash basket), I found the toadstool and handed it to Miss Switch. Then Amelia, Bathsheba, Thaddeus, and I all waited in deadly silence as she twisted and turned the toadstool in her hand, studying it in the flickering light of the Bunsen burner.

"This is it!" she exclaimed. "This is indeed a *Toadstoolius toadus reversicum!*"

"Hurrah!" cried Amelia.

"Whew! What a relief!" I said.

"Gribbet! Gribbet!" croaked Thaddeus joyfully. "But I would that *thou* couldst return me to my true self, Mistress Switch. What if thou canst not make Mordo bend to thy will?"

"We shall face that problem when we get to it, Thaddeus," said Miss Switch. "The problem we must first face is that there is only one *Toadstoolius toadus reversicum* and a large number of toads to be transformed. Fortunately, the instructions in Mordo's book state that a potion may be made by mixing the powdered toadstool in any medium, increasing the quantity considerably, and then feeding it to each subject. The question is, what to use for the medium?"

"How about some H_2O?" I suggested.

"With some $C_6H_{12}O_6$," said Amelia.

"H-two-O and C-six-H-twelve-O-six?" Miss Switch looked at us suspiciously.

Amelia and I grinned at each other.

"It's just sugar water, Miss Switch," said Amelia.

"Hmmmph!" snorted Miss Switch. "Well, I never pretended to be a scientist."

"We can get the sugar from the cafeteria," I said. "And we can bring a saucepan, too, and water. Then we can make the syrup—er—potion over the Bunsen burner.''

"And put it in some empty small milk cartons. We can get those from the cafeteria, too," said Amelia.

"Very well, you may be excused to fetch all those things while I prepare the toadstool with all the proper incantations, etc., etc." Miss Switch rapped sternly on the desk. "And please don't dawdle, children!"

"We won't!" Amelia and I promised.

Then Thaddeus croaked hesitantly. "G-gribbet! G-gribbet! Wouldst thou be kind enough to take me with thee? 'Tis most likely I may never be granted another chance to see thy Pepperdine School, or any other marvels of the twentieth century."

"Is it okay, Miss Switch?" I asked.

"Certainly! Certainly!" replied Miss Switch impatiently. "But do get on with it. We must hurry. Who knows what mischief Mordo will get into before I return."

Thaddeus hopped onto my shoulder, and after we had found a flashlight in the teacher's desk, we started off down the dark corridor. Unfortunately, when you consider what took place outside the school while we were away from the classroom, the trip took us much longer than we had planned.

I don't like to put the blame on a poor old helpless toad, but Thaddeus did ask a lot of questions. For starters, he couldn't get over our having a metal cylinder that produced a bright, steady light at one end just from our pressing a button. He also couldn't understand an endless stream of water running from a faucet, or reaching into a tall white box that stayed frosty cold all the time, and bringing out small cardboard boxes that held fresh milk. It seems hard to believe, but actually Thaddeus was more excited by all this kind of stuff than he was about television and computers. There's just no explaining some things, I guess.

At any rate, by the time we got back to the fifth-grade classroom, Miss Switch was tapping her foot with annoyance. But at least we had returned with all the stuff she needed. In short order, we had a tripod set up and had placed a mixture of water, sugar, and powdered *Toadstoolius toadus reversicum* in a saucepan over the Bunsen burner. Then, with all eyes except Bathsheba's fastened on the pan, we waited for the precious potion to brew. Bathsheba had retired to the windowsill, where she sat calmly scrubbing her whiskers.

Then suddenly, her back arched, and the fur of her tail stood out as if it had just touched an electric light socket. "Sssssssss!"

"What is it, cat?" Miss Switch asked sharply.

"Mordo's ship just flew by! Sssssssss!"

Miss Switch, Amelia, and I tore over to the window and peered into the sky.

116

"Heck, I don't see anything, Miss Switch," I said.

"Nor do I. But if Bathsheba did, that's enough for me! Never doubt a cat's eyes, Rupert." Miss Switch nudged Bathsheba. "What else did you see?"

Bathsheba gave a low growl that seemed to roll up from the tip of her tail. "Br-o-o-owl! I saw Mildew climbing up a ladder dangling from the side of the ship, and carrying one of your fifth-grade students. There were about twenty-five others already on deck."

Miss Switch's eyes grew cold and menacing. "So he's done it, kidnapped my whole fifth grade!"

"Omigosh!" I cried. "What are we going to do?"

"Not *we*, Rupert, *I*. You may recall that I promised Mordo to return without you. The two of you are going home."

"But, Miss Switch, you might need us," I said. "You're going to have to give the potion to all those jillions of toads, and keep an eye on the class at the same time." I couldn't help thinking of Billy Swanson and Melvin Bothwick, and how it took a teacher practically all her time just looking after the two of *them*.

Then Amelia tossed her head determinedly. "Besides, Miss Switch, it's our class, too, and we want to help them!"

Miss Switch hesitated. "I don't know. You're

the two Mordo is really after. It just seems too dangerous.''

"But you remember you said something was protecting *us*," Amelia reminded her.

"You sure did, Miss Switch!" I said eagerly. "Please! We want to go!"

"Oh, let them!" Bathsheba swished her tail impatiently.

"Well . . . well . . . well, all right, then!"

"Now that that's settled, Miss Switch, can we get started?" I had already forgotten how glad I was to get away from Mordo, and was burning to take off.

"Not so fast, Rupert! We have no idea if they're returning to the same place, and it would be too easy to lose them. We must be certain of their destination, and unless I miss my guess, it's to visit that *she* who seems to have Mordo under her thumb."

"Does that mean bewitching the blackboard again, Miss Switch?" Amelia's eyes were dancing.

"It does indeed, Amelia!"

And almost before you could say "Swoop! Swoosh!" Miss Switch had swept the bewitched eraser across the blackboard, and we were looking at the good ship *Bide-A-Wee,* this time sailing through the sky. It gave me the creeps to think that, all this time, the ship had been cruising around outside Pepperdine, with Mildew scurrying up and down that ladder, gathering the fifth graders from their homes. The picture took us closer and closer to the ship, over the garbagey decks and down the stairs. And there at last, in nightdresses and striped pajamas, rubbing their eyes and looking scared to death, was the whole rest of the Pepperdine Elementary School fifth grade!

"Look, Amelia," I shouted, "there's Creampuff and Banana and Billy Swanson!"

"And there's Melvin Bothwick and Betsy Cook!" cried Amelia.

"And look, look over there, Amelia, that's Peatmouse!"

"Peatmouse?" croaked Thaddeus excitedly. "Wouldst that be my descendant?"

"It sure wouldst—I mean, would!" I said.

"Quiet, children!" said Miss Switch. "What we have now is very interesting. Please pay attention!"

What we had, it seemed, was a picture of Mordo carrying on a private conversation with a witch who had the worst-looking nose in captivity.

"Gulldemonia!" I gasped.

"Yes, indeed, Gulldemonia!" retorted Miss Switch. "Now perhaps we'll find out what this whole thing is all about."

Mordo rubbed his hands gleefully. "This is splendid, simply splendid! Miss Switch's whole fifth-grade class, minus only two. What a catch!"

Gulldemonia threw back her head and cackled. "The whole fifth grade! You are clever, Mordo. *She* should be very pleased."

"*She,*" muttered Miss Switch. "So it's not Gulldemonia after all!"

"Well," Mordo said, "if you'll stay down here and see that nothing happens to this valuable cargo, I'll go aloft and help Mildew. The sooner we get to Ice Island, the better!"

"Ice Island! So that's it!" Miss Switch thumped the desk so hard it scared Thaddeus, who jumped onto my shoulder and sat there trembling.

"Wh—what's at Ice Island, Miss Switch?" Amelia asked.

"Saturna! Ice Island is the place to which she was banished by the Witches' Council for subjecting us all to that confounded Comput-o-witch. So, Saturna is the famous, or infamous, *she!* I should have guessed it."

"But how could you, Miss Switch?" I asked, patting poor Thaddeus on the head to calm him down.

"Because I knew Saturna was furious with me for being the one responsible for ending the power the Comput-o-witch held over all the witches, Rupert."

"Miss Switch," Amelia said, "why doesn't Saturna try to bewitch us herself? Why does she need Gulldemonia and Mordo?"

"That, Amelia, is because Saturna has had

most of her important powers taken away from her by the Witches' Council. I remember now that Gulldemonia was always one of her (if you'll excuse the expression) toadies. As for Mordo, I suspect she knew of his predicament, and found a clever way to make use of him as well. So, it seems there is nothing now to keep us from leaving."

Just then, however, a new problem leaped into my mind. It might not be as scary or dangerous as our forthcoming trip, but it was a big worry all the same. "Miss Switch, I don't understand why it isn't morning already, considering the time we've been gone. But it sure as heck is going to be morning before we get back this time. I—I mean, *if* we get back. My parents are going to think I've been kidnapped, too, and Detective Plume is going to go crazy. And what about Pepperdine with no fifth grade and no fifth-grade teacher?"

"Rupert, look at the clock and tell me what time it is," said Miss Switch.

I looked. "It—it's twelve thirty."

"Which is exactly the time we left for the seventeenth century. You see, Rupert and Amelia, and Thaddeus, too, we are now on witch time, which is, in a sense, no time at all. You may have heard the expression, 'I'll be back in no time at all,' or 'I'll have it done in no time at all.' Well, witch time is the root of that expression. So—" Miss Switch concluded briskly, "unless we do not get back at all, there is nothing to worry about."

I was glad to hear about witch time, but the rest of Miss Switch's statement was not too reassuring. I decided to say nothing about it, however, in case she changed her mind about taking Amelia and me.

She peered into the saucepan. "The potion appears to have cooled enough now. I have found several eyedroppers in the class first-aid kit, for administering the potion to the toads. So, if you children will now help me pour the potion into the milk cartons, we shall be off. At full broomstick speed, we should be able to reach Ice Island right on the tail of the *Bide-A-Wee*. And then," she added darkly, "we shall see what we shall see!"

12

Hurrah for Miss Switch

Ice Island! Brrrr! I can see it in my mind now, and still shudder when I think of it. All those jagged spears of ice reaching up almost to the sky and down into the dark depths, the evil glimmer of a witch's chilly moon on the deadly frozen rocks, and finally, lying in wait behind a cold curtain of giant icicles, Saturna's cave itself!

The *Bide-A-Wee* was already anchored by the island when we arrived, its tattered sails iced with frost, and icicles dangling from the yardarms. Miss Switch parked the broomstick behind a rock close to the ship. Silently, we all climbed off. It was so cold that tiny icicles were already forming on Bathsheba's whiskers. I felt something trembling inside my pocket, and reached in to give Thaddeus a gentle squeeze.

"It's all right, Thaddeus," I whispered. "I'll take care of you. And if we don't get you changed back to yourself, we'll take you with us to the twentieth century."

"Thank you! Thou art the best of friends, Rupert," croaked Thaddeus.

We moved in a silent column toward the ship, the ice snapping like brittle glass under our feet. Then we crept up the gangplank, slipping and sliding on the treacherous sheet of ice. The deck, another sheet of ice, was no easier to cross, but we made it at last to the door.

"What are we going to do now, Miss Switch?" Amelia whispered.

"I shall go down to see if Saturna is here, or if Mordo and Co. have already left. The rest of you will wait here."

"Gribbet! Gribbet!" came an urgent croaking from my pocket. "Wouldst thou lift me out, Rupert?"

I quickly fished Thaddeus from inside my jacket.

"Mistress Switch, wouldst thou please permit me to go and gather the information for thee? I am small and not easily seen, and if I am discovered, well, what would Mordo gain by turning a toad into another toad?"

Miss Switch considered this proposition for a few moments. Then she nodded. "Yes, thank you, Thaddeus. Having someone spy in advance might be very useful."

Thaddeus lost no time in leaping from my hand and hopping down the stairs. Nobody spoke as we waited for his return. Or no return, if that should be the terrible case. I believe I held my breath the whole time, until at last he came hopping back up the steps.

"I sawest nothing there but the toads," he reported.

"Which means," said Miss Switch, "that Mordo has taken his prize 'catch' to Saturna's cave. Well then, that's where we shall go!"

Amelia quickly scooped Thaddeus up in her hands. "Thank you, Thaddeus. That was very brave."

"It sure was," I agreed. "Thanks, Thaddeus."

"Oh, 'twere nothing," croaked Thaddeus. "Thou mayest put me back in thy pocket, Rupert."

I did, and felt Thaddeus trembling. He must have been scared silly. After all, if Mordo had been down there and discovered him, he might have been thrown into the cages with the rest of the toads, and been there forever. Or worse yet, he might have been thrown overboard by Mordo in a fit of rage. I gave Thaddeus another warm squeeze to let him know I understood.

We made our slippery way from the *Bide-A-Wee*, and crept to the cave. There, protected by the darkness and the curtain of icicles, we could see all that was happening inside the cave in a scene enacted by Saturna, Gulldemonia, Mordo (with a toad on his shoulder that I supposed must be Smauk the hawk), Mildew, and the whole Pepperdine Elementary School fifth grade, huddled together into one big, scared, shivering clump!

"You blithering idiot, Mordo! You fool! You lame-brained, dithering idiot! You doddering dodo!" screamed Saturna. "What in all of a witch's witchdom do you think I'm going to do with all these children? The whole fifth grade of Pepperdine, minus the only two I wanted to get my hands on. And you let those two get away! And, Gulldemonia, where were *your* brains when you encouraged him in this idiotic venture? Only two witches in the world to help me, and they turn out to be a pair of confounded dummies!"

"I—I couldn't help it," stammered Mordo. "M-M-Miss Switch—"

"Don't mention that Switch person to me!" screeched Saturna. "Over there you see the result of what happened when her sneaky little scientist student, accompanied by his sneaky little friend, fed my Comput-o-witch all that blasted nonsense about 'original witchcraft' performed by Miss Switch as a teacher. Aaaaargh! No wonder the greatest high-technology wonder of the ages lies there wrecked beyond hope of repair!" Saturna pointed a long, cruel, bony finger at a dilapidated heap of metal that certainly didn't look as if it had much of a future in the scientific world.

"W-w-well, what would y-y-you like me to do with these children?" asked the thoroughly beaten Mordo.

"How should I know?" snarled Saturna. "I trust you didn't expect me to sit around babysitting a bunch of brats. You can take them back, for all of me. What I want is those two teacher's pets, Rupert and Amelia, preferably turned into toads!"

"M-M-Miss S-S-Switch doesn't have any teacher's pets!" came a small, scared, but defiant voice from the midst of the fifth-grade class. I had trouble recognizing the voice as belonging to Peatmouse, but Peatmouse's voice it was. "She likes us all equally well!"

Oh-oh! I slapped my forehead in despair. Peatmouse had really done it!

"Likes you all equally well, eh?" Saturna stroked her hooked chin and smiled evilly.

Gulldemonia began rubbing her hands, and oozed up closer to Saturna. "There, you see, Saturna, it wasn't such an idiotic thing after all, eh?"

Saturna's eyes narrowed, and a thin, cruel smile crossed her face. "Maybe not. Mordo, since you didn't have any luck turning those other two into toads, why don't you use this bunch to practice on? And as long as you've brought them here, why don't we have a little demonstration now, eh?"

"A splendid idea, Saturna!" Gulldemonia

cackled gleefully. The warts on her ugly nose seemed to turn purple with pleasure. "Why not have him start on that one, the one who was clever enough to speak up?" She pointed to Peatmouse.

"Yes! Yes! Yes! Right away! Right away!" shouted the eager Mordo.

"Stay right here, Amelia and Rupert! You too, cat!" Miss Switch hissed at us. "This has gone far enough!" And with those words, she stepped from behind the icicle curtain and strode into Saturna's cave.

"Stop this at once!"

A startled Mordo hesitated in mid-swoop.

"Miss Switch!" gasped the fifth grade.

Saturna whirled around. *"YOU!"* she shrieked. Her eyes were raging red furnaces of fury. "What do you think you're doing here? You have no business in my cave, Sabbatina Switch!"

"Anything that has to do with my fifth-grade class is my business," replied Miss Switch coldly. "Stop what you're doing at once, Mordo!"

"No, no, don't you dare stop!" screamed Saturna. "Not if you value your miserable future!"

Mordo wasted no time. A quick calculation seemed to tell him that he had more to fear from Saturna than Miss Switch. He moved with record speed. Swoosh! Swoop! And a blinking toad appeared where Peatmouse had once stood.

"Gribbet! Gribbet!" croaked poor Peatmouse.

"Oh oh!" I whispered into my pocket. "Mordo got Peatmouse, Thaddeus. Your descendant is a toad, too!"

Right away, Thaddeus got very jumpy and agitated inside my pocket. And before I knew what was happening, he leaped out and hopped on into the cave. Without thinking, I went chasing after him. And right behind me came Amelia. And so there we all were! Except Bathsheba, the only one who had the good sense to stay where she was told.

Saturna threw back her head and gave a horrible, blood-chilling howl of laughter. "So you had those two nasty little creatures hiding outside all this time, did you? I really can't imagine why you brought them, but it was very thoughtful of you to lead them to me. Well, you've outclevered yourself this time, *Miss* Switch!"

Saturna's eyes, with pupils reduced to the size of small, cruel pinpoints, studied Amelia and me. "Mordo, it seems that you now have the key to bewitching a twentieth-century child, so go right ahead and start with the boy. He's the one I want to get first. And just try and stop this, *Miss* Switch!"

"Oh, I have no intention of doing that," said

Miss Switch cheerfully. "Go right ahead, Mordo. My pleasure!"

Amelia and I looked at each other with horror. What had happened to Miss Switch? Was she actually in league with these other witches, and had she concocted a very complicated plan to get us into this situation? I had told myself over and over that a witch was a witch was a witch, and after all, Miss Switch had been a witch long before she had ever been a teacher.

I should have thought this thing through the way a great scientist would, or even a great detective. How could I have allowed Amelia and myself to blunder into this situation? Imagine it, I had actually pleaded to be allowed to come! Well, it was too late now. Mordo had discovered the formula, whatever it might be, for transforming a twentieth-century Pepperdine fifth grader, or probably any other twentieth-century kid, into a toad. Good-bye world as Rupert P. Brown III, kid. Hello world as R. P. B. III, toad. I couldn't bear to look. I closed my eyes. But I could hear Mordo swooping and swooshing.

Swoop! Swoosh! I opened my eyes and looked down at—no, not toad toes, but sneakers. Then I looked up—at Amelia. She was looking at me. We were still the same old Rupert P. Brown III and Amelia Matilda Daley. No gribbet, gribbet. No toads. Not yet, anyway.

Swoop! Swoosh! Mordo continued, his swoops growing wider and his swooshes growing longer, and his face growing more and more frantic. Saturna and Gulldemonia began to scowl hideously. Miss Switch, on the other hand, wore a broad smile.

"Swoop and swoosh away, Mordo!" she said. "It won't do you any good. You can't bewitch either of them, no matter how hard you try."

"It's a trick!" shrieked Saturna. "Try it again. No, wait! Try one of the others first. Try that one!" Saturna pointed, and a scared Mildew quickly pulled a far more scared Billy Swanson to the center of the cave.

Now, I have to admit that I wouldn't have minded seeing Billy turned into a toad, or Melvin Bothwick either, for that matter. It would have made life a lot easier at school. Still, they were my fifth-grade classmates, and I was more loyal to them than to Saturna. I could only hope that whatever was protecting Amelia and me was protecting them, too. But if it wasn't what would Miss Switch do about it? Mordo, who had begun to look pretty unsure of himself, began to swoop and swoosh again.

"Wait!" shouted Miss Switch in a commanding voice. She pointed a stern finger at Mordo, as sparks shot from her eyes and fell hissing onto the ice.

Mordo hesitated.

"No, don't wait!" screeched Saturna. "Do, and you'll be sorry forever. I'll put you back in that little bottle and you'll *never* get out!"

"Don't let her fool you, Mordo," said Miss Switch calmly. "She's had most of her powers taken from her by the Witches' Council, but I'm sure she's never reported that to you. She could hardly get a mosquito into a bottle, much less you. If you don't believe me, let her prove it. Mildew, run back to the ship, please, and fetch the bottle."

Saturna gave a vicious, trapped snarl. "Aaaaargh! Never mind!"

"There, you see?" said Miss Switch.

But Gulldemonia gave Saturna a sharp dig in the ribs, and whispered something in her ear. Saturna smiled triumphantly.

"Do what I say, Mordo, or I'll take away your toad-bewitching powers entirely!"

Mordo clutched his throat and lurched backwards.

Before he could quite keel over, however, Miss Switch looked him dead in the eye. "I doubt that you can do any such thing, Saturna. But even if you could, perhaps Mordo doesn't care. I believe there is something he cares much more about than turning people into toads."

"Th-th-there is?" said a startled Mordo. "Wh-wh-what's that?"

"Well," replied Miss Switch, "I know you didn't like being in that bottle, but there was

134

one thing about it you liked. You liked being a captain of a ship that was all spit-and-polish, with shining brass, and spotless decks, and trim sails. And you *loved* wearing those nice, shiny boots, didn't you?''

"Oh yes, I did!" said Mordo dreamily. Then he caught himself. "But I don't want to be back in that bottle again!" he said, cringing.

"Of course you don't!" said Miss Switch soothingly. "But you don't have to be back in the bottle to have all those nice things again. You can have them right on the good ship *Bide-A-Wee,* and it can look just like it used to in that picture you have proudly hanging on your wall. You'd like that, wouldn't you?"

"Oh *yes!*" said Mordo.

"Nincompoop!" shouted Saturna.

But Miss Switch went smoothly on. "And wouldn't you like to have people trusting you again so they would come aboard to admire your beautiful ship?"

"Oh *yes!*" said Mordo. "You know, I—I *like* being the crusty, but twinkly-eyed, Captain Mordecai. I—I *like* having people like me."

"Of course you do!" said Miss Switch.

"But how can I have my shiny, spotless ship back with no crew?" Mordo began to blubber. "I've turned them into toads, and I can't turn them back again."

"Of course you can!" said Miss Switch.

Mordo's eyes popped. "*Wh-wh-what?*"

135

"Don't listen to her!" screamed Saturna. "It's all another trick!"

Miss Switch ignored Saturna completely. "What would you say, Mordo, if I told you that I have at my disposal a potion made from a *Toadstoolius toadus reversicum?*"

Mordo staggered. *"Toadstoolius toadus reversicum?* You mean the one-in-septillion *Toadstoolius toadus reversicum?"*

"That very one!"

"She's lying!" yelled Saturna, gnashing her bony teeth with helpless rage. "She can no more help you turn back a toad than I can get you into a bottle!"

"Mordo," said Miss Switch, marching right on, "which toad bewitchment would you like to reverse more than any other in the world?"

Mordo didn't have to think twice about that. He patted the toad on his shoulder. "My poor Smauk!"

"Aw-aw-awk," croaked Smauk mournfully.

"Very well, then." Miss Switch deftly pulled an eyedropper and a carton of potion from inside her cape. An anxious, hopeful Smauk dutifully opened his mouth to receive a drop of the precious potion. "You may now begin the incantations, etc., etc., Mordo," said Miss Switch.

And before you could say "bewitchment," there was one very happy warlock with one very happy hawk sitting on his shoulder.

"She be able to do it for you, master!" cried Mildew, jumping about in a manner that showed how much time he had been spending around toads.

"Now, Mordo, that is to say, *Captain* Mordecai," said Miss Switch very respectfully, "shall we return to your ship and settle the details?"

"Oh, yes, yes!" shouted Mordo, who right then, as if he didn't care to waste a moment, turned back into the crusty (but twinkly-eyed) Captain Mordecai.

Saturna and Gulldemonia, dark as two thunderclouds at their defeat, crouched beside the Comput-o-witch, glowering at this whole scene.

"As for you," Miss Switch addressed them, "if I hear of any more of these outrageous schemes, I'll see that the Witches' Council hears about it."

"He'll be sorry!" snarled Saturna. "And *you,* you'll pay for this, Sabbatina Switch!"

"I think not!" said Miss Switch briskly. "Now, come along, class."

"H-h-hurrah for Miss Switch!" a small, quavering voice sang out from the midst of the Pepperdine Elementary School fifth-grade group.

"H-h-hurrah for Miss Switch!" quavered all the fifth grade.

"Fiddlesticks!" said Miss Switch sternly. "I don't need cheers for something any good teacher would do for her class. Now we shall

137

return with Captain Mordecai to his ship, and soon you will all be home in your warm beds for a good night's sleep. You must get your rest, you know. After all, tomorrow is another school day!''

13

All in Witch Time

Well, we made it back to the ship all right, with Thaddeus riding in my pocket, and Peatmouse in Amelia's. The first thing Miss Switch did was to see that Captain Mordecai transformed Thaddeus and Peatmouse back into their true selves. Then, oh boy, you should have seen the two of them whapping each other on the back and shaking hands a thousand times. Peatmouse, ancestor, meets Peatmouse, descendant! The two Peatmouses (or I should say, Peatmice) had so much to say to each other about relatives born and yet-to-be-born, that Amelia and I finally left them to jabber by themselves. We went off to help Miss Switch herd the tired, shivering fifth grade into the old crew's quarters for the ride home.

Miss Switch told Captain Mordecai that, even though all this was happening in witch time (which, as you may remember, is no time at all), she still wanted her class delivered to their homes as quickly as possible. Since the whole class couldn't fit onto one broomstick, she just parked it aboard, and we flew back in the *Bide-A-Wee*. (This, I might add, was somewhat more pleasant than going by broomstick, since we were all inside in a nice, warm cabin.) When we arrived home, as the ship hovered above the chimneytops, each sleepy fifth grader was returned by Mildew-special-delivery to his or her room, via the ladder hung from the side of the ship.

Each fifth grader, that is, except Amelia, Peatmouse, and me. Amelia and I were needed to help with the toads, and the Peatmice hadn't had nearly enough time for their reunion. So Miss Switch allowed us to fly back to the seventeenth century. On the way, Amelia and I had the chance to ask her some pressing questions.

"Miss Switch" I said, "back in Saturna's cave, after Mordo had turned Peatmouse into a toad, how could you be so sure he still couldn't bewitch us?"

"Because, Rupert," she replied, "instant calculation told me that Mordo could bewitch Peatmouse because he had first bewitched a Partlow ancestor back in the century in which he was qualified to do his toad bewitchments. That, it seems, was the requirement for doing a descendant. First you must do the ancestor!"

"But supposing he had done some new toad bewitchments after we left the *Bide-A-Wee?*" Amelia asked.

"That wouldn't have been likely, Amelia. You may recall that Mordo and Mildew came back empty-handed from their hunting trip. For them to kidnap all the fifth grade when they did, they would have had to leave at once, so they could not have had time for further bewitching."

"Then why didn't you just let Mordo go ahead and do another fifth grader in Saturna's cave?" I asked. "You seemed pretty determined to make him stop, Miss Switch."

"Ah, that was another matter!" she said. "How was I to know that one of those toads in the hold of the *Bide-A-Wee* might not be ancestor to some others of my fifth-grade class? If I didn't put a stop to the bewitchments then, Mordo just might have figured out the secret himself."

"But even if he did, and went on turning us into toads, Miss Switch," Amelia said, "you still had the *Toadstoolius toadus reversicum* potion for him to turn us back again."

"*I*," said Miss Switch, widening her eyes at Amelia, "I could persuade him to do it. He might not have, you know. It was all a big gamble, right up to the end!"

"Whew!" I gasped. I mean, think of what might have happened to some of us if Miss

Switch hadn't been on her toes. *I* couldn't bear to think further about it.

So I didn't, because there were still other questions to be answered.

"Miss Switch, what's going to happen about the toads' remembering what Captain Mordecai did to them when he was Mordo? And what's going to happen to the fifth grade's remembering their adventure in witch time?"

"And what's going to happen when I show up at breakfast in the morning?" asked Amelia. "What's Rupert going to tell his mother and father?"

"And what are *they* going to tell Detective Plume?" I said.

"You know, Amelia and Rupert," Miss Switch replied, "I think you must have discovered by now that witches can't do everything. You have also learned that different witches have the power to do different things." She gave us a mysterious smile. "This happens to be one problem I can take care of very easily. But no more questions. We have a great many things to do."

The great many things, of course, were helping feed the magic potion to Mordo's gigantic collection of toads. But it was then we found out at least part of what Miss Switch's mysterious smile was all about.

When the sailors and village residents were returned to their natural selves, they rubbed their eyes and acted as if they had just awakened from a long, deep sleep. The sailors all appeared to be terrifically embarrassed about the condition of the ship, and got to work cleaning it up at once. The villagers all seemed to be embarrassed at being caught out so late, and slunk off the ship in a great hurry to get home. Not one of them remembered a thing about being a toad, or Mordo ever having been anything but the crusty (but twinkly-eyed) Captain Mordecai!

At any rate, with the toads taken care of, it was time for us to leave on the broomstick. Naturally, the Peatmice didn't want to part company.

"Thou canst not depart when I have just discovered thee," wailed Peatmouse, seventeenth century.

"Well, I don't want to go!" cried Peatmouse, twentieth century.

"Why dost thou not stay here?" asked P. 17th cent.

"Why dost, I mean, why don't you come with me?" asked P. 20th cent.

"I cannot leave my mother and father," groaned P. 17th cent.

"I can't either," moaned P. 20th cent.

Sadly, the Peatmice decided they had to stick with their own centuries. Then there was a lot more handshaking, promises to remember each other forever, and even to write letters. It occurred to me that this latter would be slightly impossible to do, but I didn't want to add a sour note to this already melancholy occasion.

Captain Mordecai and Mildew, who was now a captain's aide decked out in a smart new sailor's uniform, also didn't want to part from us.

"You be never able to see the Cap'n's shiny, shipshape ship," said Mildew tearfully.

"Oh, we have a picture of it in our history book," I said, "so we know exactly how it's going to look."

"And we'll admire it every day when we have our history lessons!" Amelia promised fervently.

"Avast and belay, but that will be splendid!" said crusty (but twinkly-eyed) Captain Mordecai, with a catch in his throat.

"You be a good boy and girl," said Mildew.

"Aw-aw-awk!" said Smauk.

It was, all round, a very sad parting.

Were we to have another sad parting with Miss Switch? She said nothing when she left us off at my window (after depositing Peatmouse at his) except to tell us that she wanted us both in bed and asleep in no time at all. Amelia and I couldn't help smiling when we looked at the clock on my wall. It was exactly 12:30 A.M., witch time!

The next morning began just about like any other school morning of my life. My mother had to yell up the stairs three times before I appeared at the breakfast table. The only difference this time was that Amelia was there ahead of me, and so, naturally, was held up as a model of timeliness and perfection and cleanliness and anything else destined to make us enemies for life, except that it didn't work out that way. I like Amelia despite all those qualities. But what I am trying to say is that there was no mention of kidnapping or disappearing or anything like that. It was just as if it had never happened. Good old witch time! I thought.

On the way to school, we passed Detective Plume on *his* way to work. Then I did something that wasn't too bright. I smiled at him. It turned out all right, though. Detective Plume smiled back, but in a sort of nervous, surprised way, as if he wondered who I was, and was I maybe a little balloony to be so happy to see someone I didn't even know.

As for the fifth grade, they all looked pretty tired, and some of them had drippy noses. But nobody was talking about any trips to Ice Island on a flying ship and meeting up with some witches. This is certainly something you would think a person would be talking about, if they remembered.

Peatmouse raced over to tell me about this weird dream he had about meeting some ancestor of his who was also called Peatmouse.

"Golly," I said, "maybe it wasn't a dream. Maybe it really happened."

"Broomstick, you'd better go cool yourself on the monkey bars!" Peatmouse said, which was kind of disappointing. It was better that the rest of the fifth grade didn't remember anything, but I guess I did sort of want Peatmouse, twentieth century, to remember Peatmouse, seventeenth century. Still, you can't have everything.

That disappointment, however, was replaced by a far worse one. Instead of Miss Switch at the teacher's desk, there sat ordinary, medium-old, fuzzy-red-haired Mrs. Fitzgerald. The only thing is, I guess I halfway expected it. After all, Miss Switch had done what she came to do, which was rescue Amelia, and then had done a lot of other rescuing besides. And I knew how she felt about all that sentimental nonsense, as she would put it. But it was a terrible blow, and I couldn't help feeling she should have said something to Amelia and me before she left, the way she did the last time.

Then, midway through the morning, Mrs. Fitzgerald called me up to her desk. "I just found this note for you, Rupert. It seems to be from Miss Switch. Probably something to do with your handwriting. She really worries quite a bit about it."

The note inside the envelope was actually to me *and* Amelia. This is what it said:

146

"Dear Rupert and Amelia,

After all the excitement of the winter holidays, school always seems a little dull and dreary, even with the best teacher in the world. But just remember this, that spring will be here *in no time at all!*

Miss Switch"

Amelia and I are going to keep this note forever. Also, we are both certain Miss Switch was trying to tell us that, one day, she would return to Pepperdine. In the meantime, though, we spend a lot of time looking for a certain toadstool so that we won't have to wait too long. The other day we happened to find two pretty interesting ones. These are the notes I made about them in my private notebook:

What:	Toadstools
Kind:	*Toadstoolius summerium vacationus perpetuum Toadstoolius nomorius homeworkium*
Whose:	Pepperdine Elementary School's
Performance:	None to date
How Tested:	No known way to prove scientifically

Neither of these, of course, is the one we are looking for, which happens to be a *Toadstoolius Miss Switchius returnicum*. But Amelia and I intend to keep on looking, even if there is only one in ten centillions. We do not give up easily.

I guess this about concludes my report, except that, as a scientist, I feel I should present some proofs that all this actually happened. As a matter of fact, I do have three.

The best one, unfortunately, has turned out to be a disappointment. That's our fifth-grade history book. Oh, the picture of Captain Mordecai's ship is there, all right. But even with the strongest magnifying glass, you can't find the words *Bide-A-Wee* printed anywhere. But that's witchcraft for you, and you'll just have to take my word for it that the words were once there.

Another proof is the old oak tree in our backyard. You can see where a branch has been torn off, the one that Mordo (now the crusty, but twinkly-eyed, Captain Mordecai) used to fly Amelia back to the rocky coast of Maine in the seventeenth century. My mother and father always wondered how that branch could have just blown right out of our yard. Naturally, I have never told them.

As for final proof, you may remember that when Amelia and I heated the bottle that held Captain Mordecai (formerly Mordo), the cork popped out. Well, I found that very same cork hidden in a dusty corner of my room, and now have it mounted and hung over my desk with this legend printed under it, CORK—17TH CENTURY. Needless to say, my father (the great humorist) finds this very amusing. But I don't say anything. I just look at him, and smile.

ABOUT THE AUTHOR
AND ILLUSTRATOR

BARBARA BROOKS WALLACE was born and raised in China, where her father was stationed on business. She came to the States to attend Pamona College and UCLA, and later married Lieutenant Colonel James Wallace, Jr., of the Air Force. They now live in Virginia with their son.

Miss Switch to the Rescue, the sequel to *The Trouble With Miss Switch,* has enjoyed popularity both as a novel and as a two-part, animated ABC "Weekend Special."

KATHLEEN GARRY MCCORD is a free-lance illustrator and printmaker. She teaches book illustration at the University of California at San Diego.